Nothing cha
despair.

Finn was exact
and the effect he had on her was just the
same. She stood transfixed, desperately
trying to swallow the lump in her throat as he
threaded his way surefootedly over the rocks
towards her.

She couldn't move, her feet rooted to the
sand, but it didn't matter because he came to
her anyway, moving with an easy grace as he
sprang lightly down off the rocks and came
to rest a few feet away.

'Janna.'

Just the one word, but it took her breath
away.

Caroline Anderson's nursing career was brought to an abrupt halt by a back injury, but her interest in medical things led her to work first as a medical secretary, and then, after completing her teacher training, as a lecturer in Medical Office Practice to trainee medical secretaries. In addition to writing, she also runs her own business from her home in rural Suffolk, where she lives with her husband, two daughters, mother and assorted animals.

Recent titles by the same author:

LOVE WITHOUT MEASURE
TAKEN FOR GRANTED
ANYONE CAN DREAM
ONCE MORE, WITH FEELING

A FAMILIAR STRANGER

BY
CAROLINE ANDERSON

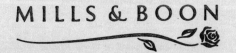

MILLS & BOON

For James and Fiona; Jessie and Celia; Alastair and Rhea; and all the kids in the phone box.

*MILLS & BOON, the Rose Device and
LOVE ON CALL are trademarks of the publisher.
Harlequin Mills & Boon Limited,
Eton House, 18-24 Paradise Road, Richmond, Surrey TW9 1SR
This edition published by arrangement with Harlequin Enterprises B.V.*

© Caroline Anderson 1995

ISBN 0 263 79359 1

*Set in Times 10 on 11½ pt. by
Rowland Phototypesetting Limited
Bury St Edmunds, Suffolk*

03-9510-45513

Made and printed in Great Britain

CHAPTER ONE

'HE'S back, you know.'

Janna paused, her hands on the bandage motionless but for a small, almost undetectable tremor. It wasn't necessary to say who 'he' was—Finn's return to the fold was the talk of the community, and it seemed everyone was delighted.

Everyone, that was, except Janna. As far as she was concerned it was a disaster of monumental proportions. She tore off a piece of tape and secured the end of the bandage, then answered, 'So I hear. You'll be glad to have him home after so long.'

'Oh, aye,' Jessie McGregor agreed with a wistful sigh, and then added, 'I doubt I'll be alone.'

Janna met her eyes at last, her own wary, and saw understanding and sympathy, and something else—something that could have been a plea.

She put on Jessie's stocking and stood up, brushing her hands over her skirt to distract from their trembling.

'It's over, Jessie. It scarcely started, but it's been over and done with for years.'

'Over it might be, but done with? I think not, lass. Certainly not for Finlay, and not, I think, for yoursel' either.'

Janna cobbled up the paper bag with the old ulcer dressing in it and busied herself tidying.

'You're wrong, Jessie. Finn's a friend now. Nothing more.'

'If you say so, my dear,' Jessie said calmly, setting her foot back on the ground and struggling into her slipper. 'Now, how about a nice cup of tea?'

Janna always had a cup of tea with Finn's mother, but just now, today, she thought she would choke on it. Anyway, Finn could walk in at any time. . .

'I won't, thank you,' she said hastily. 'I've still got more to do—visitors to go and see—and it's Dr MacWhirter's farewell do tonight, so I mustn't be late.'

She stooped and kissed Jessie's soft, smooth cheek, then, gathering her things, she left, closing the door softly behind her and resisting the urge to run to the car and drive off into the sunset.

Instead she set her bag carefully on the floor of her old diesel runabout, slid behind the wheel and turned the ignition. It was difficult, she reflected wryly as it clattered to life in a cloud of black smoke, to flee romantically in something as down-to-earth as Betsy!

She headed back towards Port Mackie and her next call, several miles away over the indifferent roads and twisting, hilly terrain. She would have preferred a four-wheel drive vehicle, rather than the sensible little runabout so suitable for her city colleagues, but district nurses in the Highland region didn't get allowances that stretched to Discoverys or Shoguns, even though they often needed something more robust.

Janna was lucky. She could have had a newer car—even the Discovery that would have been perfect for the job—but her grandmother's legacy sat patiently in a building society account, waiting until Janna was able to buy her dream house. Then and only then would she spend her carefully hoarded money, although she was often tempted to replace Betsy, especially in the winter.

There were times when Janna thought she spent longer in the car, wrestling with the difficult terrain, than in her surgery or with patients, but every time she was tempted she thought of the barn in Camas Ciuicharan and the house it would become if only old MacPhee would sell, and so she struggled on with the old rattletrap. At least it was reliable.

Anyway, the time spent in the car was in many ways a bonus. The countryside was beautiful, and she was happy with her own company. Solitude gave her time out from the pressures of life, and allowed her to find a measure of contentment—a contentment that was just now feeling sorely threatened.

She saw her patient: a visitor to the area with a bad head and a touch of gippy tummy from too much haggis and ten-year-old single malt—an unhappy combination. All he required was a sachet of electroyte replacement and a little sympathetic reassurance that he wasn't going to die, and then Janna was able to head home.

She didn't go straight there, though, turning off instead for Camas Ciuicharan—the Bay of Laments.

It had got its name from the sighing of the wind between the rocks, supposedly a Highland lass mourning the death of her loved one, and it suited Janna's mood exactly. Here was where she would live, in the little barn with its wonderful views over the sea, and only the sheep for company. There was another car there, a dark green Discovery with Edinburgh plates, but no sign of anyone in the bay. Probably a holidaymaker gone for a walk. She parked her car beside it, then strolled down over the grassy dunes on to the rocks of the foreshore.

A small crescent of clean white sand lay curved in

the lee of the bay, and the crystal-clear water was turquoise in the sunlight. It looked inviting, as it always had. Many times she had swum here with Finn and the others in her childhood, and again that summer. . .

With a quick glance round to make sure she was alone, she slipped off her shoes, wriggled out of her tights, tucked up her uniform skirt and walked knee-deep into the water. It was cold, of course, being the North Atlantic, but blissfully refreshing, and for a mad moment she considered ripping off all her clothes and diving headfirst into the gently lapping waves.

It wouldn't have been the first time, but now modesty forbade her—modesty and a very real appreciation of what such a scandalous act would do to her reputation in this very tight-knit and highly moral Highland community. Once she hadn't cared, to her parents' utter humiliation, but she was, after all, no longer fifteen, and it was still broad daylight!

With a sigh of regret she turned back along the beach, paddling at the water's edge and staring out across the sea at the islands floating in the low mist that swept across the water. A little sloop was moored in the bay, rocking gently in the swell, its mast gilded by the sun. She could hear people talking and laughing on board, their voices carrying clearly in the still, clean air.

She loved the evenings here, the glorious colours of the sunset, the changing sea and sky, the gradual dark-ness that enveloped the pleated land and laid it to rest.

A ripple of laughter came to her over the water—the occupants of the boat enjoying each other's company.

A sharp stab of loneliness pierced her, and with it dread. How would she cope with Finn's return? He had meant—still meant—so much to her. Did he have any idea how hurt she had been by his casual dismissal of their love?

It had been seven years ago, and they were both older and wiser now. Would it hurt less? She didn't think so. Jessie was right, it was over but it wasn't done with. Not by a long way—at least not for Janna. Finn had left it behind him years ago, which was the trouble, of course. If only she could let it go too, perhaps she might heal, but the pain of his rejection and indifference was with her daily. They could have had so much, and yet they had nothing, their love swept aside by his sudden and inexplicable return to their long-standing friendship.

He had come back at Christmas, months after her birthday, after their loving, after his promises, and had treated her exactly as he always had, as if the summer had never happened. She had been so shocked and hurt that she had avoided him all that holiday, and ever since she had gone out of her way to avoid him.

Well, she wouldn't be able to now. They were stuck with each other, working together, and she was going to have to put on the acting performance of her life to survive it.

For a long time she stood motionless, staring out over the water, and then with a sigh she turned and walked back towards the rocks.

As she did so she felt a sudden prickle of awareness and glanced up. There was nothing there, of course. It was just because she was thinking of him, in this place which had been so special to them that summer. She was conjuring his presence out of thin air, an extension of her night-time fantasies, her dream lover come back to haunt her. And yet the prickle was still there. . .

She scanned the area again. Nothing. All she could

see were the sheep, grazing around the ruins of McPhee's derelict barn—the barn where she and Finn had lain together seven years ago and promised each other eternity.

Then she saw him, silhouetted in the doorway, tall, broad, his dark hair touched with red by the sun, an old T-shirt stretched over his broad shoulders, tucked into snug jeans, faded and ancient and clinging lovingly to his narrow hips and long, lean legs. Nothing changes, she thought in despair. He was exactly as she remembered him, and the effect he had on her was just the same.

She stood transfixed, her heart thrashing in her chest, desperately trying to swallow the lump in her throat as he threaded his way surefootedly over the rocks towards her.

She couldn't move, her feet rooted to the sand, but it didn't matter because he came to her anyway, moving with an easy grace as he sprang lightly down off the rocks and came to rest a few feet away.

'Janna.'

Just the one word, but it took her breath away. His voice hadn't changed at all—deep, soft, slightly husky, it sent shivers racing over her skin and turned her resolve to mush.

With a superhuman effort she dragged air into her lungs and met his clear blue-grey eyes, navy-ringed around the iris and able to see clear through to her heart—or so she had once thought. They hadn't seen her pain, though, so apparently they were just ordinary eyes after all, if one discounted how incredibly beautiful they were. . .

'Hello, Finn.'

He studied her for a moment, his head tipped

to one side, and then clicked his tongue.

'You've lost weight.'

She gave a strained little laugh. 'I needed to.'

'No.' He shook his head. 'You were perfect just as you were. Oh, Janna, it's good to see you again.'

Without warning he took the last step forward and enveloped her in a huge, bone-cracking hug. Her nostrils were assailed with the familiar scent of his skin, and for a second she allowed herself the luxury of returning his hug, her arms sliding round his big ribcage, her hands involuntarily flattening against his smooth-muscled back.

His body was warm under her palms, warm and lean and solid, bigger even than she remembered. She ached to hold him, to stand there in the shelter of his arms and hang on for dear life. For a moment, it almost seemed as if they were lovers again, as if her love was returned by the man in her arms. . .

She was deluding herself. Dropping her hands back to her sides, she straightened away from him. He let her go, his large hands cupping her shoulders and holding her at arm's length while he studied her face, his own creasing in a frown.

'You look tired,' he told her bluntly.

'I am. It's the height of the summer season. All the visitors are here, and we seem to have a particularly stupid lot this year.'

Laughter touched his eyes. 'They can't be that stupid. They chose the most beautiful place in the world to have their holidays.' He released her and turned towards the sea, gazing out as she had done, his eyes reflecting the islands and the changing clouds in the sky. 'I've missed it so much—the sea, the gulls, the people—and you, Janna.'

She swallowed and turned away, refusing to be lulled by the sincerity in his voice. 'Me?' she said with a fragile laugh.

'Does that seem so strange?' he asked softly.

Strange? Why should it be strange that he should vow to love her for all time and then forget about it for seven long, aching, miserable years until it was convenient to amble back into her life? Did he really expect her to believe he had missed her? Hardly, surely!

And, just because he was back, did he imagine they could pick up where they left off?

'It's been a long time, Finn.'

'Twelve years since I left.'

And seven since their summer. 'I've changed,' she told him.

'I would hope we both have. That doesn't mean we have to forget the things that were once important to us.'

Did that include her? Her heart, always the optimist, jerked against her ribs, but then common sense reasserted itself. No, she was just simply available, a passably attractive woman—and an old lover, to boot—still unattached in an area where there were only a handful of young people and most of those still at school. He wouldn't be human if he didn't try to take advantage of her availability. Janna knew that, just as she knew how easy it would be to turn back to him, to hold out her hand, to lead him up the hill to the barn and there——

No! She wouldn't allow him to use her as a convenience—even if he did only have to crook his little finger before she wanted to run to him.

Bending, she scooped up her shoes and tights.

'I have to go—another visit on the way home,' she lied.

'Will I see you at Bill MacWhirter's do tonight?' he asked.

She stopped in her tracks. Of course, he would be there too. He was taking over from the old doctor. From now on he would be everywhere. Every time she turned round or looked up or breathed in, he would be there. Could she cope?

She would have to. She would be strong, and hold him at a distance, and then he would leave her alone. He must. Please, God, he must. . .

'Yes,' she told him evenly. 'I'll be there.' Then she walked away, and with every step she could feel his eyes burning into her spine.

As she reached the car he called her name.

She turned back towards him. 'Yes?'

'If you're going on a visit you might want to do something about your skirt,' he said with a grin, and she glanced down to see with horror that her skirt was still tucked into her knicker-legs like a little girl's. Blushing furiously, she tugged the thing down and slid behind the wheel, dusting the worst of the sand off her feet before shoving them into her shoes without the tights. It didn't matter. There was no visit, anyway.

Hands shaking so badly that she could scarcely fasten her seatbelt, she started the car and drove a little way, before pulling over and sagging over the steering-wheel with a sigh of frustration. How was she going to cope with him? He would drive her crazy—that megawatt charm and wicked, wicked grin undermining all her good intentions.

'Damn you, Finlay McGregor,' she muttered.

'Damn you for coming back and messing up my mind!'

Shoving the protesting lever into first gear, she swung back out on to the road without checking her mirror. There was a screech of rubber, and the unmistakable tinkle of breaking glass.

She stopped, her heart sinking, and got out.

Finn was just climbing out of the cab of a dark green Discovery with Edinburgh plates, propped gently against a rock by the side of the road.

'Trying to run me off your territory, Janna?' he asked mildly.

She gathered her wits. 'Are you all right?'

'Aye—by a miracle. That and the fact that I was already slowing down to see if you were all right. I gather you're not, or you wouldn't be driving like that.'

She started to shake. How could she have been so careless? If only he hadn't come back. . .

'It's your fault,' she told him unreasonably. 'You taught me to drive!'

He grinned infuriatingly. 'So I did. Clearly I have only myself to blame. Perhaps you'd better go on to your next visit and I'll follow at a safe distance.'

She drew herself up. 'You do that—give me half an hour's start!'

'I intend to,' he said drily, and got calmly back behind the wheel and reversed back on to the road, then got out again to check the damage.

'Send me the bill,' she called back to him.

'My pleasure. Now, perhaps we'd both better move so John-Alec can go about his business?'

Janna looked up and saw the farmer in his Land Rover, waiting patiently up ahead of her. She muttered a rude word under her breath, started her car and left the explanation to Finn.

'So, Janna, what do you think about this young scallywag, grown up and taking my place, eh?'

Old Bill MacWhirter had an arm flung affectionately around both Janna and Finn, and she found it impossible to avoid seeing Finn's mouth soften in a smile.

'Scallywag, sir?' he challenged.

'Scallywag. Best damn salmon poacher I ever met—barring your father as a young man, God rest him.'

Finn chuckled. 'There were more than enough fish.'

'Oh, aye, laddie, and you were a joy to watch, the way you could tickle them almost into a coma.'

They all laughed, Janna politely and a little distractedly, because she was remembering the first time Finn had kissed her, lying on the banks of MacWhirter's burn and laughing while her first tickled salmon trout flapped beside them on the bank. 'Clever girl,' he'd said, and then suddenly the atmosphere had changed and he had leant over, his cool, wet fingers steadying her chin as his mouth lowered to taste hers. She had been fifteen, and Finn twenty, fully grown, her childhood idol turned with a single kiss into the subject of her adolescent fantasies. . .

'So, Janna, answer the question. It can't be a surprise to you.'

She shrugged. 'He always said he'd be back,' she said simply. 'I hear he's a good doctor—no doubt our patients will be quite safe. They seem happy enough.'

'And what about you?' the old doctor asked.

Janna laughed. She wouldn't be safe—not by a long way. Finn haunted her every waking moment, and joined her in her dreams. No, she wouldn't be safe, and for that reason she couldn't allow herself to be happy. 'I dare say I'll make the best of it,' she replied lightly, and was surprised to see a flicker of hurt in Finn's eyes before he disguised it with a laugh.

She felt a softening, a weakening of her resolve, and excused herself to slip outside and spend a few overdue minutes shoring up her defences. If she allowed herself to start feeling sorry for him she was lost, and she knew it.

No, Finn had been the transgressor, Finn the one who had turned his back on their love, and Janna was damned if she was going to let him back into her heart on the strength of one tiny flicker of hurt.

She closed her eyes and leant back against the wall, inhaling deeply to soak up the mild, dark night. Why had he come back? Her life was tolerable here, empty of love, but full in many other ways.

Damn him, she had been content until today. Now she was a seething mass of confusion.

The hair prickled on the back of her neck, and she opened her eyes to see him standing a few feet away, watching her thoughtfully.

It didn't surprise her that she hadn't heard his approach. For all he was a big man, he was lighter on his feet than anyone else she had ever met. Nor did it surprise her that she had known he was there. She had always had a sixth sense where Finn was concerned. She spread her hands out over the wall behind her, drawing strength from the rough-hewn stone of the old schoolhouse.

'Are you OK?' he asked softly.

'Why shouldn't I be?'

She saw his big shoulders shrug slightly in the gloom. 'No particular reason. You looked a little strained, that's all. I wondered if you were ill.'

He moved closer, the grass whispering under his feet, and stood just inches away, so that the scent of his soap teased her nostrils and caused an ache low down in her body—an ache only Finn could cause, or ease.

His hand came up, fingers curved so that his knuckles brushed lightly over her cheek. Her lips were suddenly dry and she tucked them in, running her tongue over them and then standing, mesmerised, as his thumb caressed their soft fullness, dragging gently on the newly moistened surface.

A tiny moan rose in her throat, and then it was too late to protest because his body, warm and hard and strong, was cradling hers as his mouth came down and settled against her lips in the softest, gentlest caress.

She wanted to cry out, to wrap her arms around him and hold him close, to draw him down with her on to the soft grass and let her love take its course, but some vestige of common sense made her stand still, silent and unresponsive, as his lips sipped and brushed and cajoled.

She ached to open to him, to taste him again, to see if he was still as sweet and potent as he had been that long, hot summer. His tongue swept over her lips, probing gently, and she felt her knees threaten to give way. But she couldn't give in—she mustn't.

She turned away slightly and the pressure eased, leaving her empty and unfulfilled as he lifted his head, his expression veiled by the dimming light, but she heard him sigh softly as he stepped back.

The silence stretched, broken only by the muted laughter from the building behind them and the fragmented sound of her breathing. 'Why did you do that?'

she asked in a strangled whisper. 'Why couldn't you leave things alone?'

He sighed again, a deep, ragged sigh full of regret. 'I'm sorry. I didn't come out here with the intention of kissing you. Forgive me, Janna.' His hand came up to cup her cheek, but she jerked her head back and hit it against the hard stone of the wall.

A little cry escaped from her lips, and then his gentle fingers were in her hair, finding the tiny abrasion and soothing it with whisper-soft caresses that made her want to put her head down on his chest and cry.

He tutted gently, her name a breath on his lips, teasing her hair. 'Silly girl,' he soothed, but it didn't soothe her, just made the need to cry even stronger.

'Why are you doing this?' she wailed softly into his shirt. 'Why can't you leave me alone? Why did you have to come back?'

'You knew I was coming back,' he said. 'It was hardly a secret.'

She gave a rude snort and pulled away, more cautiously this time. 'No. And, of course, you always keep your word.'

'I'm here, aren't I?' he replied, irritation colouring his voice. 'Damn it, Janna, what am I supposed to have done wrong?'

'Done?' she exclaimed, her hands pushing feebly at his massive chest. 'Apart from vanishing for years and then coming back and expecting me to be all over you like a rash? Get real, Finn!'

He sighed again and released her, ramming a large hand through his hair and ruffling the already unruly locks. 'What do you want from me, Janna?'

She bit her tongue to stop the plea from coming

out. 'Nothing,' she said instead. 'Nothing at all. Why should I?'

Finn sighed again, turning to stare out across the sea, gleaming in the last rays of the late sunset. 'I thought there was something between us once.'

'There was—seven years ago. That's rather a long time to carry a torch, Finn.'

He turned back towards her, his eyes hooded and unrevealing in the dusk. 'I had no job, no clear idea of where I was going to live. You were just starting your training—anything between us would have been impossible then.'

'You said you were coming back,' she mumbled.

'I'm here, aren't I?'

'It took you long enough—and what about all the time in between?' She straightened up, moving away from him in case she gave in to the urge to throw herself into the comfort of his arms, and made herself meet his eyes again. 'You can't really expect to disappear from my life so comprehensively and then waltz back in as if you own me!'

'I didn't disappear! Every time I've been back while you were here you've had to go away, or been busy, or some feeble excuse. I haven't been avoiding you, Janna, you've been avoiding me! It's hardly my fault if I finally took the hint and left you alone.'

Was that true? Had she driven him away herself? Was it possible she'd really read him all wrong? Perhaps the change in him that Christmas hadn't been so significant; perhaps he had been just the same old Finn that he always was, even though he'd been her lover.

No. He had been different before her birthday, before he went away. Perhaps he'd just regretted it.

Her father had talked him out of his impulsive urge to marry her on the spot—perhaps his arguments had been too convincing?

Janna sighed. 'Maybe we just took each other for granted, Finn.'

'So what now, Janna?' He reached out for her, then dropped his hands and rammed them into his pockets. 'Look, we can't talk about this here. Let me take you home when this do is over, so I can talk to you, just for a while. There's a lot we need to say.'

'I hardly think that will look very good—you coming home with me your first day back.'

He laughed. 'With your parents standing guard like chaperones? Not even in this part of the Highlands are they that fanatical about propriety.'

'What have my parents got to do with it? I don't live at home any more. I haven't for the past year.'

He looked astonished. 'Where do you live, then?'

She waved over her shoulder. 'There—the Nurse's House, of course.'

He shook his head as if to clear it. 'I'm sorry, I just assumed——'

'Well, you shouldn't, Finn. You shouldn't assume anything about me any more—nothing at all. And now, if you'll excuse me, I have to go and see off our guest of honour.'

Drawing in a steadying breath, Janna tipped up her chin, straightened her shoulders and somehow found the strength to walk away.

That Friday night signalled the end of Janna's hopes that working with Finn would mean a return to the easy, casual relationship of their childhood.

Once she had resented that treatment from him—

now, perversely, she longed for it. Finn, however, obviously had something more in mind, and Janna didn't know how to deal with it. So she took her usual action in the face of Finn's inconstancy—she avoided him.

On Monday morning Finn took the usual branch surgery, held at the Nurse's House in Kilbarchan, and although he said nothing Janna could see from his eyes that he wanted to talk to her and wouldn't rest until he had.

Fine. She wasn't at all convinced that she was strong enough to deal with him once he really turned on the charm, and dragging up all her old fears and disappointments would upset her. The last thing her pride needed was Finn reducing her to tears of disappointment and confusion. What a weapon!

No way was she handing him that on a plate. She was polite, courteous, but distant—and out of a room whenever he entered it.

It worked—to a point. By eleven-thirty, however, he'd had enough, and came and tracked her down in her room where she had just finished with the last patient.

'All done?' she asked brightly.

'No, I've got to put some stitches in a nasty leg wound—one of our visitors slipped on a hill path this morning on the dewy grass and cut his leg on a bit of old rusty iron sticking out of the ground. I wondered if you could give me a hand?'

She nodded. 'Of course.' At least with the patient between them things couldn't get too personal, she reasoned.

She had reckoned without her response to his presence. It was enough that Finn was in the room. He

didn't have to look at her or talk to her or touch her—
all of which he did, of course, while he was working.
Nothing personal, all strictly professional, but it was
enough to drive her to distraction.

Finally they were finished, and Mr Gibbs was asked
to come back on Wednesday to have the stitches
checked and the dressing changed.

Janna quickly cleared up, then headed back to her
room, leaving Finn organising a prescription to be
delivered that afternoon from the dispensary at the
main surgery in Craigmore.

She was about to escape when he reappeared in her
doorway, lounging comfortably against it and cutting
off her retreat.

'What now?' she asked, a little shortly.

His eyebrows rose. 'Sorry, am I holding you up on
your visits? I just wanted a word about Betty Buchan.
She seems to be getting more and more confused.'

'She is,' Janna agreed. 'Her neighbours worry about
her, but they keep tabs on her and let me know if they
think anything's wrong. She reports to them daily on
the phone.'

'If she could remember what time of day it was,'
Finn said drily. 'I gather she woke the shop in the
middle of the night again to order her groceries.'

Janna had heard about that. It was getting more
difficult to see the funny side of Mrs Buchan's confusion now, and Janna was increasingly worried about
the elderly lady's safety.

'I'll go and see her again,' she told Finn quietly. 'I
think it's maybe time she went into some sort of care.
I'll see if I can persuade her.'

'Won't her family mind if you interfere?'

'What family?' Janna scoffed. 'They don't give a

damn. Someone has to take responsibility, and her family won't.'

'Or can't?'

'Won't,' Janna said firmly. 'Is there anything else?'

'Yes—Janna, have I got something contagious?'

Her smile faded. 'Contagious?' she said in mock innocence. 'You tell me.'

'Janna, stop it. We need to talk.'

'No, Finn,' she corrected, 'you need to talk. What I need is to get on with my rounds. Please lock the door on your way out.'

And with that she walked away from him for the third time. She wondered how many more times she would get away with it.

Not many, she suspected—not unless he had changed even more than she imagined.

CHAPTER TWO

THE day was one of quiet, routine visits for Janna, interspersed with the usual forgetful tourists. Appalled to discover that the nearest chemist was over an hour away by car, they rang the nurse.

'I've left my drugs behind, dear, and I can't possibly ask my friends to take me all that way,' one lady told her, and then it transpired that she couldn't remember what they were all called. 'Those funny little pink and white ones—you know. And some yellow ones with something written on them.'

Janna had to call the patient's GP in Manchester and sort out a repeat prescription, then phone the surgery at Craigmore to get them to make up the drugs and send them out with the next delivery.

Another family of visitors had a child with tummy-ache. Janna called to find that the father and two younger children had gone out for a walk on the beach, and the mother and Julie, the little girl with the pain, were quietly reading a book.

Not, Janna thought, what most little girls would want to do on a beautiful sunny day. She looked pale and pasty, and Janna's first instinct was appendicitis. However, the pain didn't seem bad enough, so Janna asked a few questions about the origin of it. Apparently it had been there off and on since just before they left, and the mother reported a history of 'nervous' tummy-ache in the child.

'She hates change, and I wondered if she was worried

24

about coming up here. She's had to leave her rabbit with a friend and it's been fretting her, and sometimes she gets tummyache just from worrying,' the mother explained.

Janna examined her, asked about problems with passing urine, or if she had constipation or diarrhoea, took her temperature and pulse and found them more or less normal.

'Are you worried about anything, Julie?' Janna asked her.

The little girl nodded slowly. 'My rabbit,' she said.

Janna turned to the mother. 'Could you ring the people looking after her, so Julie can reassure herself? Perhaps that really is all that's wrong.'

'Oh, dear, I feel so silly,' Mrs Harvey said apologetically. 'I didn't mean to waste your time, but she did look so pale.'

'She is pale, and I don't mind you calling me out. You did entirely the right thing, Mrs Harvey,' Janna soothed the young mother. 'We never mind coming out to a child with tummyache or earache. However, this time I really think it's probably nothing much to worry about. Just keep an eye on her, and if you're still worried give me a ring later on and I'll get the doctor to pop in and have a look at her before tonight, OK?'

With a smile and a wave to the wan little girl on the sofa, Janna left them and went to old Mrs Buchan.

She came to the door in her nightdress and dressing-gown, looking faintly surprised. 'It's you, hen — I wondered who was calling in the middle of the night. Come away in — it's awful late, but I dare say we could ha' a wee dish o' tea.'

'Mrs Buchan, it's lunchtime,' Janna told her gently. 'See, the sun's high in the sky.'

She squinted over Janna's shoulder, her brow creased in confusion, and then her eyes filled and she turned away. 'So it is. Come away in anyway, hen, it's nice tae see you just the same.'

Janna followed her in, shaking her head slightly. Poor old thing, if only she hadn't started to lose her mental faculties she would be fine on her own, because her body was still fit, honed by the harsh life and fresh air. The little croft was simple but spotless, and as Janna followed her into the kitchen she wasn't surprised to see freshly baked bread out on the side.

'Had to bake ma own bread—the shop didnae have any.'

At four o'clock on a Monday morning, Janna reasoned, they probably wouldn't have had.

'Mind,' she added, 'Moira was cross wi' me because I woke her up from a wee nap—fancy that, Janna, having a nap in the shop in the middle of the afternoon!'

'I thought it was night-time, though?'

Her brow creased. 'So Moira said.'

'You're getting in more and more of a muddle, aren't you, Betty?' Janna said kindly.

Old Mrs Buchan sighed shakily. 'I never seem to be able to work out the time—I've one of those clocks wi' twenty-four hours, but I cannae work out the time on it. And in the summer the nights are so short, and I seem to doze in the day. Everything just gets in a grand old muddle, and then I make a nuisance of mysel' and folks get angry——' She broke off, biting her lip, and Janna put her arm round the slender shoulders and gave her a hug.

'Don't fret, Betty. You're not a nuisance, pet. I think I'll have a word with Dr McGregor and see if you should have something to help you sleep at night— that way perhaps you'd get back into a pattern of sleeping at night and being awake in the day, and it would help you to work out what the time was.'

She chatted for a few more minutes with the lonely old lady over a cup of tea, then headed back to her house to grab a late bite of lunch and check her phone for messages.

There was a note from Finn in his jagged, powerful scrawl.

Dinner tonight at the hotel at seven. I'll pick you up at ten to. Be here, please. Finn.

The 'please' was underlined about a dozen times, and Janna's heart sank. Evidently he meant to talk to her.

She checked her answerphone, found a call she needed to make to an elderly patient at Inverbeg, and set off again.

'Mac' McDougall was an old man, housebound, and supported by a team of carers and auxiliaries, and Janna had already visited him that morning. He was restless, however, and had apparently pulled his catheter out.

'What've you been up to, my darling?' she asked cheerfully as she prepared the necessary equipment.

'Are you cross wi' me, Sister?' he croaked.

'No, Mac, you've just been a bit silly. You must leave it in, otherwise you wet the bed. Let me see you, now.'

She peeled back the bedclothes and found his pyjamas were soaked and so was the bed. First things first, she thought, and stripped him out of his wet things, washed him down and started on the catheter. Once he was leakproof, she decided, she'd tackle the bed.

Inserting a new catheter was a job Janna did often, and she wouldn't have minded at all except that Mac was rather difficult to deal with and refused to keep still, bending up his legs and rolling over so that Janna had to start again twice before she managed to insert it and fill the balloon with saline to keep it in place— not that the balloon had stopped him pulling the last one out.

She could see that his urethra was a little sore as a result, and so she had used plenty of anaesthetic jelly on the new catheter; by her third attempt it must have been numb enough not to worry him any more. However, she was feeling harassed, the procedure had taken far longer than it should have done, and she was worried about little Julie Harvey.

'There—now, please, Mac, leave it alone, my dear.' She taped the end of the catheter firmly to his thigh, so he couldn't get hold of it too easily, and then helped him into dry pyjamas, remade the bed in double-quick time and popped him back in.

Already it was nearly four, and as she had to pass the house she called in on the Harveys.

'Oh, she's much better now she's found out that the rabbit's OK,' Mrs Harvey said blithely. 'She's gone down to the beach with the other two.'

For some reason Janna didn't feel reassured. 'Call me if you're unhappy or the pain comes back,' she repeated, and went back to the Nurse's House.

One last maternity check, she thought, and then she was off duty and could get ready for dinner with

Finn. The young woman she had to visit was eight months pregnant with her third child, and Janna was trying to persuade her to go to Inverness or Fort William the following week, to be on the safe side. Her first two labours had been protracted, and without the prompt attention of the maternity staff at Inverness could have had a much less happy outcome.

However, against all advice, Lindsay Baird had decided to have this baby at home. Dr MacWhirter's opinion on the subject had been pithy in the extreme, and his parting shot to Janna on Friday had been, 'Well, at least I don't have to be responsible for the Baird delivery now!'

Janna, however, was, in her capacity as community nurse and midwife. If Lindsay refused to go to hospital and had the baby at home, technically Janna was absolved if anything went wrong. Morally, however, she knew she had to do everything in her power to get the woman to listen, even if it mean worrying her to death with what might go wrong in order to make her take advice.

She arrived at the house and found Lindsay lying in the garden on a sun-lounger, enjoying the warm summer sunshine while the children played in the sand-pit beside her. She greeted Janna with a wave. 'Hi—grab a seat.'

'I will—fancy a drink?'

'Oh, love one. The kettle's hot.'

Janna made a pot of tea and took it out to the garden. Lindsay was one of her contemporaries, and Janna knew her well. It helped, because it meant that she could take a more frank approach.

'I don't suppose you've come to your senses?'

she asked bluntly as she poured the tea.

Linday shook her head. 'Janna, I really want a normal, natural birth. I'm sure the others were so traumatic because I wasn't at home. If I was here, and relaxed, it could all be so different.'

'Lindsay, that's hogwash. Of course being relaxed helps, but it won't increase the diameter of your pelvic outlet. You're small, your husband's big, and you suffer a degree of pelvic disproportion every time. When was your last scan?'

Lindsay sighed. 'Three weeks ago, and they said it was almost as big as it could get.'

'Well, then.'

'Well, then, nothing. Janna, I want to have my baby at home!'

'Even it if means risking its life?'

'Janna, don't be melodramatic! I'll be fine, I know I will. I'm confident.'

'Did anybody ever tell you were stubborn?' Janna asked mildly, giving up for now.

'Me?' Lindsay snorted. 'Never. Tell me, how's Finn? We missed MacWhirter's party on Friday, so I didn't see him. Is he still as gorgeous as ever?'

'Are you changing the subject, Lindsay?' Janna asked, trying to ignore the soft colour flooding her cheeks.

'Yes,' her friend replied, eyeing her blush with interest. 'Are you?'

'Yes.'

'Nice weather for July.'

'Isn't it?'

'Janna?'

'Mmm?'

'Are you still in love with Finn?'

Janna stirred her tea absently. 'Why would you think that?'

'Because I know you. You look strained.'

'Finn said that.'

'He's right.'

'So am I—Lindsay, you can't have that baby at home.'

'I can.'

Janna sighed. Why was everybody so determined to be difficult today? She left Lindsay, still adamant about a home birth, and went home to examine the sparse contents of her wardrobe. Heavens, there were still things in there Finn would recognise! Still, it was only the local pub they were going to, and she was damned if she was going to try and impress Finn! She dug out a silk shirt, jeans, and a newish sweater in case it got chilly later, showered in double-quick time and arrived in the hall just as the bell rang.

Carefully arranging her face into a non-committal smile, she opened the door expecting Finn, and found instead Sue, the landlord's daughter. 'It's Julie Harvey,' she said frantically. 'They were in the pub having supper and she keeled over. She looks dreadful! You must come!'

Janna picked up her bag, scribbled a note for Finn and stuck it on the door, and ran down the road after Sue. By the time she arrived at the pub Julie had been put into a little back room, and had been violently sick several times.

'Oh, Nurse, thank God you're here,' Mrs Harvey said fervently. 'I can't understand it—she was so much better.' And she started to shake all over.

Moving her gently out of the way, Janna looked at

the little girl's flushed face and glazed eyes, and took her temperature.

'It's up now, quite a bit,' Janna told the girl's mother. 'I think she's got appendicitis, but Dr McGregor will be here in a minute and he'll confirm it. It's all right, sweetheart,' she said gently to the little girl as she was sick yet again. 'You'll soon be OK. We'll look after you.'

Just then she heard Finn's deep, soft voice, and he came into the room, glanced at the child and then at Janna, and raised his eyebrows.

'Appendix, I think,' Janna told him.

He nodded, examined her quickly and turned to the parents. 'Yes, it looks like a classic appendicitis, so she'll need to go to hospital straight away, and I imagine they'll operate as soon as she arrives. I'll go and make the arrangements.' He went out to the bar, and a few minutes later came back with a little towel— wrung out in warm water. 'They're on their way,' he told everyone generally, then crouched down by the little girl on the bed, wiping her face and hands gently with the damp towel. 'Can you hear me, sweetheart?'

The little girl opened her eyes and nodded, a shiver running through her.

'Julie, inside your tummy there's a little thing like a curly tail, called an appendix. Have you ever heard of it?'

She nodded, her eyes wide. 'A boy in my class had one of his out.'

Finn suppressed the smile. 'Well, sweetheart, I think you might have to have yours out, too, because I think it's gone bad, and it's making you feel poorly, isn't it?'

She nodded again, her eyes filling with self-pity. 'I feel ever so sick,' she whispered.

'I expect you do, poppet. Now, tell me, how do you fancy going in a helicopter?'

Her eyes rounded. 'A helicopter? I've never done that before.'

'Not many people have—and I bet when the boy in your class went to hopsital to have his appendix out he just went in an ordinary ambulance, didn't he?' Julie nodded. 'Well, you're going to have something to tell him when you get home, aren't you?'

She smiled faintly, and Finn squeezed her hand and straightened up, turning to her mother and father.

'You will have gathered the air ambulance is on its way from Inverness—it'll be here in about half an hour, and it will be able to take Julie and one other person.'

'Inverness!' Mrs Harvey exclaimed. 'Isn't there a hospital closer?'

'No. Well, there is, but it takes longer to get there by road, and I think time is of the essence. Your little girl's pretty sick, Mrs Harvey. You don't want to waste time.'

As the significance of Finn's comment sank in, Mrs Harvey collapsed on to a chair, her face ashen. 'Is she really that ill?' she asked. 'I thought she was just worrying about the rabbit!'

'I'm afraid not.'

'Is it critical that she's hospitalised so fast?' Mr Harvey asked Finn. 'It will make visiting them so difficult. Can't they deal with something so common here?'

Finn shrugged. 'They can, of course. I could take out her appendix myself with anaesthetic cover. However, I don't have it, and although it's a common complaint it can be quite serious if it's neglected or if treatment is delayed. She'll be fine once she's had her appendix out,' Finn assured them. 'I just don't think you want to jostle her about on the road unnecessarily in case it perforates. Now, will one of you be going with her? You might just have time to get a few things together before they get here.'

Mrs Harvey looked at her husband. 'I'll go—can you find us a change of clothes and wash things?'

With a nod he left, and a few minutes later they heard the steady beat of the helicopter rotors. Within minutes Julie was strapped to a stretcher, Finn had handed over to the team doctor and they were loading Julie and her mother into the helicopter in the field behind the pub. Mr Harvey returned in the nick of time and handed a bag to his anxious wife. 'I've probably put in all the wrong things,' he told her.

'It doesn't matter. Take care of the other two—come up and see us tomorrow.'

'I will. Ring me.'

He hugged her briefly, then Finn led them all back out of the way and the helicopter roared into life, the steady wop-wop-wop of the rotors fading gradually into the distance.

Mr Harvey, one arm round each of the two younger children, turned to Finn. 'Will she really be all right?'

'I'm sure she will,' Finn said confidently. 'Don't worry—the helicopter seems very dramatic, but it's just a case of distance and terrain. People round here soon take it for granted.'

He nodded. 'OK. Thanks. Will it be all right to ring the hospital later on?'

'Of course—try them about ten o'clock. OK?'

'I'll do that. Thanks again. Come on, kids, let's get you home to bed.' As Mr Harvey led the other two children towards his car, Finn turned to Janna.

'Well, hi there,' he said with a smile.

She laughed softly. 'Hi.'

'Hungry?'

'Starving.'

'When aren't you?' Finn said with a laugh. 'You were hungry the first time I met you, and as far as I know you've been hungry ever since. Come on, let's eat.'

'Can I clean up first? Julie was in a bit of a mess. I could do with a change of clothes.'

Finn sniffed, and grinned. 'Good idea. I could do with a wash, too. I'll walk you back to your house.'

'Such a gentleman.'

'Don't knock it.'

On the way, people seemed to come out of the woodwork and find them.

'McGregor! Good tae see ye!'

'Finlay—my, laddie, you're even bigger!'

'Caught any salmon yet this season, Finn?' This last with a dig in the ribs from Auld Jock, a friend of Finn's late father.

'I'll see you in a minute,' Janna mouthed over Jock's head, and left him to it.

She heard him come in through the front door while she was changing into an older pair of jeans and a sweatshirt that had definitely seen better days. Oh, well, So much for trying to please Finn. It was the last thing she should be doing, anyway. Perhaps it was a blessing Julie Harvey had been sick on her clothes!

He appeared from the cloakroom just as she stepped down into the hall. His eyes swept over her, softened in a smile and his hand came up and cupped her face. It was cool from the water and sent shivers over her skin. 'OK now?' he murmured.

'Fine,' she told him, annoyed with herself because her voice was breathless and thready. What a fool!

'Let's go, then.'

She felt the firm, warm pressure of his hand against the small of her back as he ushered her out of the door and down to the street, but just when she was ready to protest they had crossed the road and his hand fell away.

She felt the loss of contact right down to her socks. Damn you, Finn, she thought. Why can't I get over you?

'Come on,' she said brightly. 'I'm starving, and they've got venison casserole on the menu. I'd hate them to sell out.'

'Always your stomach,' Finn grumbled gently, but he let her lead the way, and for most of the meal she managed to stall the inevitable confrontation. In fact, for a while, she even thought she'd imagined there was a confrontation coming up.

She hadn't. Finn asked for their coffee on a tray and took it outside, led Janna to a bench under the old horse-chestnut tree and turned to her as soon as they were seated.

'We've got a problem, Janna, haven't we?' he said without preamble, handing her a cup of coffee. 'I hoped we'd be able to work together well, but you don't seem very happy to see me. I don't know why you've been avoiding me, but clearly you've got your reasons. Do they mean we can't work together now?'

She stared blankly at the swirl of cream circling slowly on the dark coffee. The prospect of losing him again suddenly overwhelmed her, and her hand trembled. 'Of course we can work together, Finn,' she said quickly. 'We're both adults. We're capable of being sensible. I'm sure we'll be fine.'

But her cup rattled betrayingly against the saucer and she put it down sharply, folding her hands together in her lap to steady them.

Finn reached out his hand and covered them, his thumb idly caressing the inside of one wrist. 'I'm sorry if my coming back has messed things up for you, Janna. I didn't intend to stir up old hurts or interfere with new relationships. I thought we were still friends.'

Janna couldn't look away, transfixed by the searching, gentle eyes that she loved so much. She felt her own eyes welling, and blinked hard to stop them. 'Of course we're still friends,' she whispered, and then his face blurred and she closed her eyes.

'Ach, Janna,' he groaned, and pulled her gently into his arms, folding her against his chest and cupping the back of her head with one large, comforting hand.

'I've missed you,' she mumbled into his jacket.

'I've missed you, too, Janna,' he replied softly, and she wondered if she'd really heard the wistful tone in his voice, or if her desperate heart had simply imagined it. . .

After that things were easier. Finn didn't try to kiss her again, and in fact he seemed to go out of his way not to crowd her.

Perversely, she found herself missing it, and wished he wasn't being so gentlemanly and reasonable. It was, however, wonderful to spend time with him again, albeit sporadically. He was very busy, and they only met on Monday morning, Wednesday morning and Friday afternoon at his surgeries. Otherwise she only spoke to him on the phone if she had a worry about a patient, and although she was busy she found the hours spent in the car between patients left her altogether too much time to dream.

Lindsay Baird was worrying her, and she spent a long time on the phone to Finn on the Monday evening of his second week, discussing her case history and how they could best manage her labour should the need arise. Janna was growing more certain that it *would* be necessary to manage her labour, because the woman was quite steadfast in her refusal to go to hospital.

'Lay it on the line,' Finn told her.

'I have.'

He sighed. 'Have you got any midwifely textbooks that show obstructed labour and describe the consequences?'

'Finn, don't you think that's a bit drastic?' Janna reasoned.

'We've got to do something if she steadfastly refuses to see sense. I'll come over and visit her tomorrow. Maybe she'll listen to me.'

'She wouldn't listen to MacWhirter.'

'He's too nice. I won't be.'

Janna sighed. 'Finn, don't frighten her unnecessarily.'

'Janna, someone has to. It might as well be me. She can't have the babe at home.'

However, by the time he got to see her on Tuesday, after his surgery at Glenmorriston, Lindsay's labour was already established.

Finn returned to the house and reported to Janna, and they sat in her kitchen over a cup of tea and discussed where to go from there.

'What stage is she at?' Janna asked, watching Finn toying with a biscuit.

'Dilating steadily—about four centimetres when I was there—and I don't think she had any intention of calling you until it was too late to do anything. Regardless, she's quite determined not to go to hospital. She threatened to sue me if I called the ambulance.'

'And you listened?'

He grinned. 'I always listen when people talk about suing me!' The grin faded, and he reached for another biscuit, snapping it in half and dunking it in his tea thoughtfully. 'I don't know, Janna, she's not due for two weeks, and the baby's head doesn't seem that big. I'm almost tempted to let her try.'

'Finn!'

'I know, but maybe she's right, Janna. She's much more relaxed and comfortable at home, and with proper management and support she might well be fine.'

'And if she's not?'

He shrugged. 'It's academic, because the damn girl won't go in, anyway. And, whatever we think, it's her decision. We can only advise.'

Janna sighed. 'What does Fergus think now?'

Finn laughed. 'He's talking about how he's going to spend the life insurance.'

Janna was scandalised. 'How can you both joke about it, Finn? She could die—certainly the baby could!'

'Aye, well, perhaps. But I think it's unlikely. I'm sure we'd get her in before that if we could really convince her there was a problem.'

Janna rolled her eyes. 'Brilliant.'

He grinned again, that wicked grin she had fallen in love with at the age of two or thereabouts—probably younger. 'Think of it as a challenge,' he said cheerfully. 'How's your midwifery?'

'Fine, as far as it goes, but I'm not Jesus. There's a limit to my talents.'

His big hand came across the table and cupped hers reassuringly. 'Don't worry, Janna, she'll be fine. We'll get her through.'

Six hours later Janna was beginning to doubt Finn's confidence and her own sanity. Lindsay was struggling, Fergus was frantic, and Janna was worried to death.

Finn, on the other hand, was quietly encouraging, and still taking a positive attitude in the face of Lindsay's stubborn determination.

'I can do it—I know I can,' she muttered, but the pain and effort were beginning to exhaust her.

Janna was worried because the pressure of the baby's head was causing bruising and soft tissue swelling, which was only serving to obstruct her labour further.

She took Finn on one side.

'That baby has to come out soon or it won't come out at all! She's not going to manage without forceps, Finn.'

'Yes, she will,' he said calmly. 'We'll get her up and moving again.'

'Finn, she's beyond that,' Janna reasoned.

'No. The baby's not distressed yet, and Lindsay's still determined. We'll have that baby out in less than half an hour, Janna, I promise.'

'And if you don't?'

'I'll use the forceps.'

Their eyes locked. Slowly, almost imperceptibly, like a wild fawn he had nursed one spring, Janna felt her tension ease. She could trust him. More importantly,

Lindsay could trust him. He would never do anything to harm her.

Janna nodded. 'OK,' she agreed, and together they went back into the bedroom. Lindsay was dozing and Fergus was sitting on the edge of the bed holding her hand, his eyes closed. As they approached he lifted his head and looked at them.

'Well?'

'We need to get her up, Fergus. She's not going to get anywhere like that,' Finn told him.

'She's exhausted.'

'She'll do. Lindsay?'

Her eyelids fluttered and she looked blearily at Finn. 'Come back tomorrow,' she slurred. 'Too tired now.'

'No, you're not. Come on, I want you walking around.'

'Can't,' she mumbled.

Finn didn't bother to argue. He pulled back the covers, slipped an arm round her waist and hauled her to her feet.

'Finn, no,' she moaned, sagging back.

'Do you want the forceps or the helicopter?' he threatened gently.

She bit her lip, straightened her legs and stood up again. 'I'll walk,' she said, and, leaning her weight on him and Janna, she trailed slowly up and down the bedroom, pausing after a few moments for a contraction.

'I want to push,' she told him.

'Not yet. Come on, let gravity help you.'

'I can't!' she cried out, reaching for her husband, and he put his arms round her and glared at Finn.

'Let her lie down!'

'No,' Finn said calmly. 'She has to stand and keep

moving as long as possible. We could do with some encouragement, Fergus,' he added, the gentle admonishment bringing a slight flush to his old friend's cheeks.

Still, it did the trick. Fergus encouraged, Finn and Janna supported, and together they walked her round and round through several more contractions.

Then Janna knelt on the floor and examined Lindsay, who was finding walking difficult by now because the head, against all odds, was finally descending.

Unfortunately the baby's heartbeat was also dropping with each contraction, and only picking up to a limited extent afterwards. That worried Janna, and she met Finn's eyes with a troubled look.

'We need to move a bit quicker,' she said economically. 'The head's well down now, but she'll have to hang and squat to get the maximum pelvic capacity,' Janna told him, and so they led her back to the bed, sat Fergus on the side, with Lindsay facing him between his legs and hanging round his neck, and together Finn and Janna directed her pushing and breathing until the baby's head was crowning at the entrance to the birth canal. Please, God, let us be in time, Janna prayed.

The perineal skin, already damaged by the two previous difficult deliveries, was beginning to look hopelessly overstretched, but still it held, delaying the birth.

'Do you want the scissors?' Janna asked Finn softly, but he shook his head.

'No.'

'She'll tear,' Janna warned in an undertone.

'Quite likely,' Finn said calmly, but there wasn't time

to wait and do a nice, tidy episiotomy with the scissors. Using his big fingers to brace her perineum, he waited for the next contraction, ordered Lindsay to push gently with her mouth open, to soften the power of the push, and caught the baby's head with his other hand, rendering Janna not only redundant but speechless.

Not only had Lindsay not needed forceps, but she wouldn't need stitches either, and the baby, if the yelling was anything to go by, was fine.

Her eyes prickling, Janna supported the baby as Finn turned Lindsay and sat her on the floor between Fergus's feet, and then she handed the little girl to her exhausted but ecstatic mother. She held the baby to her breast, and immediately the crying stopped, replaced by the steady, rhythmic sound of suckling.

'I said I could do it,' Lindsay told them victoriously, and Finn, the tension gone, sat back on his heels and sighed.

'Don't ever—ever!—pull a stunt like that again, Lindsay,' Finn warned. 'You came that close to losing her.' He held up his finger and thumb a fraction apart, and Fergus shuddered.

'Don't. Lindsay, you are a stubborn, stupid woman, and I'm having a vasectomy as soon as I can get one.'

'Oh, you're only cross because you don't get to spend the life insurance,' she teased, but her eyes were misted and so were his.

Finn shook his head. 'Daft, both of you. Right, Lindsay, let's get you on the bed, get this placenta delivered and then tidy you up. I've got twenty miles to drive before I can go to bed, and it's already after midnight.'

In fact, by the time they were able to leave

the Bairds it was nearly two, and Janna, thinking purely practically, found herself suggesting on the way home that he should stay the rest of the night with her.

'After all, you've got a surgery here in the morning, so it seems silly to go all that way, especially as the calls are being transferred to my house anyway.'

'Are you sure it's a good idea?' Finn asked her.

She wasn't, not at all, but the offer was out now and it seemed silly to try and retract it.

'I think it's an excellent idea,' she said. 'It's too late to drive back now—what a waste of time.'

'I was thinking of your reputation,' he told her quietly.

'Oh, stuff. We're professionals. Anyway, nothing's going to happen.'

His smile was wry. 'We know that, Janna, but what about the busybodies in the village?'

'They're asleep—or they should be. Don't worry.'

He was silent until they were in the house, then he turned to her again as she hurried across the hall with an armful of sheets, heading for the stairs. 'Janna, are you sure about this? I don't want to compromise you.'

She laughed. 'Finn, where you're concerned there's nothing left to compromise. Of course I'm sure.'

He followed her into the spare room, his brows crawling together in a frown. 'What are you talking about? We never did anything that would damage your reputation.'

'No?' She laughed again, flapping out a sheet and spreading it over the mattress of her spare bed. 'What about poaching MacWhirter's salmon trout? And riding down into Port Mackie on the crossbar of your bike at about thirty miles an hour and crashing into

Mrs Cameron's front garden when your brakes failed? And what about the time MacPhee caught us all skinny-dipping at Camas Ciuicharan?'

'All of those little stunts were your idea!'

'So? You were with me. Everyone thinks you led me astray!'

He threw her that devastating grin across the bed, his shadowed cheek dimpling with mischief. 'OK, OK, your reputation's in shreds. I'm sorry. As it's clearly too late to worry, yes, please, I will take you up on your offer.'

He smoothed the sheet, tucked it in and took the quilt from her, threading it deftly into the cover while she dealt with the pillowcases.

'Cup of tea?' she offered, patting the pillows straight.

He shook his head. 'No, thanks. I really am dead tired. If you don't mind, I'll turn in now.'

'I'll get you a towel,' she said, and hurried past him, ignoring the urge to put her arms round him and thank him for saving Lindsay's baby.

Moments later she returned with a towel, a clean flannel and a new toothbrush. 'Here.'

He took them from her, his manner quietly courteous but dismissive, and with a muttered goodnight she left him and went to her room, closing the door and shutting it firmly behind her.

What did she want, for goodness' sake? Was she expecting him to drag her into bed and make love to her?

A sudden stab of need caught her by surprise, and she sat at her dressing-table, yanking out hairpins and brushing her dark hair out over her shoulders while she glared at her reflection. Her eyes, usually greeny-grey, looked back at her like exhausted smudges in her pale face. No wonder he hadn't dragged her to bed, looking like that.

Smacking the brush down on the dressing-table, she pulled off her clothes, tugged her dressing-gown on and belted it firmly, then went to the bathroom. She washed quickly, scrubbing her teeth and dragging a hot flannel over her face, before opening the door and walking smack into Finn's chest.

She stepped back, an apology on her lips, and found herself staringly longingly at the broad expanse of warm, silky skin lightly dusted with soft curls between the open edges of his shirt. She'd seen it before, a million times, so why was she so fascinated by the way the hair changed direction and made that little whorl just over the flat, copper nub of his left nipple? Or by the silken texture of his skin, gilded by the light from the bathroom that streamed over her shoulder and touched him with gold? Or by the way the hair arrowed down, a fine line of soft, dark down that disappeared so intriguingly——

She yanked her eyes up and they locked with his, and for an endless moment they stood there, trapped in the silence of the night, conscious only of the empty house and the beating of their hearts.

Then with a muttered apology Finn stood back and let her pass, and she fled to her room, her heart hammering, the blood roaring in her veins, and her whole body quivering with a need she didn't dare to name.

CHAPTER THREE

WHEN Janna came down the following morning—
safely washed and dressed—he was gone, his bed
neatly stripped, the sheets in the washing-machine, and
a note propped up against the kettle.

Morning! I'll be back at eight-thirty—breakfast
would be terrific. Finn.

She opened her fridge and gave its meagre contents
a jaundiced sneer. Terrific? Somehow she didn't
think so.

She glanced at her watch. Eight-fifteen. The shop
would be open, and she just had time.

Moira loomed large and imposing behind the bacon
counter, slicing ham for the tourists' sandwiches.

'Morning, Janna!' she called. 'I had a feeling ye'd
be in after your busy night. What can I get ye, hen?'

Janna's heart sank. She might have known Moira
would be up to date with the night's activities! Oh,
well, she was here now. There was nothing for it but
to be civil and brazen it out. After all, nothing had
happened. Hopefully, she wouldn't know that Finn had
stayed the night.

'Morning, Moira. Some bacon would be lovely, and
a few tomatoes and some eggs—oh, and I'd better
have some fresh bread. I think mine's a wee bit past
its sell-by date!'

'Hungry after his busy night, eh?' Moira asked, as

casually as a circling shark, as she slapped some best back bacon down on the scales.

Why had she come in here? Janna asked herself, helplessly casting about for a sane answer. She was saved by a gruff, slightly husky voice behind her.

'Aye—I'm starving, Moira, and I thought I'd talk Janna into cooking me breakfast. Lindsay Baird had her baby.'

Moira gave him a level look. 'Aye, I'd heard about the bairn and your busy night at our end of the peninsula,' she said pointedly. 'Well, just so long as that's all you talked our lassie here into.'

Finn grinned disarmingly, his darkly shadowed jaw adding to his wickedly sexy looks. 'Moira, don't you trust me?'

She snorted. 'Only as far as I can throw ye, laddie.' She set the half-dozen fresh eggs down on the counter, and brushed her hands off on her ample hips. 'So, how's the wee'un, then?'

'Gorgeous,' Finn told her easily, and, flipping out his wallet, he paid for the shopping, scooped up the bag and held his arm out to Janna. 'Come along, Janna. I'm dying of hunger here.'

She gave his bulky frame a withering look, flashed a last weak smile at Moira and preceded him out of the shop, trying to ignore the feel of his warm, hard hand on the small of her back.

'Morning, Finn. Morning, Janna,' a voice called.

Finn's mouth tipped. 'Morning, Mrs McAlister. Lovely day.'

The elderly gossip leant on her broom and squinted at the sky. 'Aye, it's going to be a guid one. So, how's the wee bairn?'

Her, too? Janna thought. Behind her back she felt

Finn's hand keeping up a steady pressure, propelling her gently across the road to his car.

'Doing well,' he answered, without breaking his stride. 'We can't stop, we're going up to see them again just as soon as we've eaten breakfast.'

'Aye, well, you feed him up, Janna—he's had a busy night,' she said, with what Janna could have sworn was almost a leer on her wrinkled face, and then turned her attention back to her broom.

Janna sighed quietly. Hadn't anyone in the village slept last night? Beside her she heard Finn chuckle, and the temptation to kick him almost overwhelmed her.

Still, that was unfair. It had, after all, been her idea to let him stay the night. It just hadn't been one of her better ideas.

'Never again,' she muttered under her breath, but he heard her and chuckled again.

'Ach, Janna, they're just a clutch of nosy old hens. Pay them no attention.'

He held the car door for her, dumped the shopping on her lap and then swung himself up behind the wheel. The engine roared to life and Finn pulled smoothly away, leaving the old hens behind. Janna leant her head back against the head-rest and sighed.

'Tired?' His voice was soft, concerned, the voice of a friend, and Janna felt herself crumple inside.

'A bit.' She turned her head towards the window and gazed sightlessly out. Did she really want to be his friend? The answer was more complicated than a straight yes or no, of course. She wanted more from him than that—much more. She wanted what she had once had, what he had promised and then snatched away.

The only trouble was that love wasn't part of the

current package. All he wanted from her was a co-operative colleague—and, if she had any sense, she wouldn't consider offering him anything more. He had hurt her once. What was to stop him doing it again?

Nothing.

It was a painful thought, but it kept her on the straight and narrow.

She cooked his breakfast while he showered and dressed, and when he reappeared, clean-shaven and smelling of soap, she felt a pang of regret.

Idiot! What was she thinking about?

Not the breakfast. Finn rescued the bacon in the nick of time, elbowed her out of the way and cooked the eggs and tomatoes himself, allowing her to put bread in the toaster and make a pot of tea. While the kettle boiled her eyes strayed to his back, studying the broad shoulders, the narrow waist and lean hips, the neat, firm bottom above those long, impossibly sexy legs. He moved, the fabric shifting against his thighs, and she shut her eyes and turned away. What was she thinking about? She must be nuts, standing here with him in the kitchen and eyeing him up. She had to work with him, for heaven's sake! She couldn't afford the luxury of her hormones.

'Who was the call to?' she asked him now.

'Mac McDougall. He'd pulled his catheter out again, but he'd made himself so sore I couldn't put another one in. I stuck a bag on instead. You'll need to go and give him a look later. I think, to be honest, he could do with going to Craigmore to the nursing home for a while, just until he settles down again. Do you want your eggs turned over?'

'Yes, please. Why do you want him admitted? He won't get better—in fact, if he goes in I doubt he'll come out again. Anyway, he won't go.'

Finn flipped the eggs out of the pan, slid the tomatoes off the slice and set the plates on the table. 'Has anybody tried?' he asked.

Janna laughed. 'Only about a hundred times. He won't leave the house, and there's no one to look after him except me and Social Services. He has three home helps during the course of each day, and I visit him each morning and do his pressure areas and check his catheter—he's beginning to break down, no matter how careful I am, but we can't afford a ripple bed for him and he won't lie on the sheepskin.'

Finn sighed, slathering butter on a piece of toast and tearing off a chunk with large, even teeth. 'Damn fool.'

'He can't help it,' Janna defended gently. 'He's going senile, Finn.'

'Aye, I know. I'm sorry, I just see all the burden falling on you.'

'That's fine. That's why I'm here, because I'm needed. If it wasn't for Mac, and others like him, I'd be working in the city instead of being out here in the middle of the Atlantic at the end of a two-hour drive!'

Finn's mouth lifted in a smile of understanding. 'I can't argue with you, Janna. This bacon's lovely, by the way. Is it from the smokehouse at Inverbeg?'

She nodded. 'Moira gets it every week.'

'It's good,' he mumbled round another mouthful.

Janna watched him, distracted for a moment, then turned her attention to her own meal. After a moment she looked back at him. 'Finn, I'm glad you're home. I'm worried about your mother.'

He shot her a crooked grin. 'Were those two remarks connected, or are you telling me something?'

Her heart thumped. 'Don't be silly. Of course they're connected.'

'Hmm. So, were you trying to shift responsibility for the treatment of my mother's leg ulcer from yourself to me?'

She shook her head helplessly, unable to stop the smile. 'Really, Finn, you are the limit. Of course not. I just wanted to talk to you about her.'

His smile did funny things to her insides. Leaning back, his big frame making the chair creak slightly, he wrapped a large hand round his cup and watched her over the top. 'What about her?'

Janna shrugged. 'She's lonely since your father died. I know she's busy with the Lunch Club, and helping with the Seniors, but in the six years since he died she's been so empty inside. It worries me.'

He nodded. 'Yes. It worries me, too.'

'It's lonely here,' Janna went on, 'very isolating. In the winter there's nothing to do, and often she can't get out because of the weather. It depresses her.'

Finn looked stunned. Such was his love for the place, he couldn't imagine anyone ever being depressed on the peninsula. That his own mother might be was almost inconceivable.

'It's beautiful here,' he said slowly. 'I would have thought it would comfort her.'

'And maybe it would, if she was young and fit and happy, and had a reason to be alive.'

He shot her a sharp look. 'Are you saying my mother doesn't have a reason to be alive?'

Janna nodded. 'That's exactly what I'm saying, Finn. She's lonely, she has nothing significant to live for— if it wasn't for the Lunch Club I think she would have withered away long ago.'

Finn stared hard at his hands, locked together on the edge of the table, the knuckles white. 'I knew she was unhappy,' he said slowly, 'but I never realised it went this deep. I should have seen it. I thought she was better—getting over him.'

Janna reached out and covered his hands with hers. 'Maybe she'll pick up now you're back at home, Finn. She's missed you, you know. . .'

He looked up and met her eyes. 'And you, Janna? Have you missed me?'

If you only knew, she thought with a stab of pain.

'We've all missed you,' she compromised, but her voice was soft, and Finn's searching gaze must have seen the love in her eyes.

Quickly she pulled her hands away. 'I'd better go and check on the Bairds, or it'll be time for surgery and I won't be back. You don't really need to come, do you?'

He followed her out of the kitchen in a thoughtful silence. She reached the door and pulled it open, but he was still standing in the hall watching her, hands thrust deep into his pockets, his eyes hooded and unrevealing. 'Running, Janna?' he said softly.

She felt a quickening of her nerves, a tiny flash of panic at being found out. 'No, not at all. By all means come. I was just trying to save you time,' she lied.

He laughed, a soft, humourless huff of laughter in the quiet hall. 'You're right. I'll stay here and sort things out ready for the surgery. You don't really need me there. I was just coming to have a cuddle with the baby. Give them my best.'

With a nod she went out, pulled the door shut behind her and almost ran to the car. It was ridiculous, she thought as she started the car and headed for the hill behind the town and the new baby that needed her attention. She was going to have to do better than that to keep her distance from him.

It was difficult, though, because whenever she was near him she found her mind starting to wander and her brain curdling like Mrs Buchan's. Perhaps, if she tried really hard, she would be able to check Lindsay and her child without forgetting what she was doing. It was unlikely, though. The way Finn made her feel, she had difficulty remembering her own name!

It was a busy morning. She helped Finn with the surgery, changing dressings where necessary, doing inoculations and smears and blood pressure checks. She ran an ECG on Mrs Linley, and noticed there was a marked arrhythmia. She smiled at the woman, asked her to get dressed and wait in the hall, and went in to Finn with the result after his patient came out.

'Mrs Linley—she's got a definite arrhythmia.'

He frowned at the trace, running the tip of one strong, blunt finger along it. Janna couldn't take her eyes off the finger—or the hand it was part of. Strong, lightly dusted with hair, it was the hand of a powerful man, a man at home in this wild and rugged country that she loved. She ached to reach across the desk and take that hand and cradle it against her heart, so he could feel the erratic beat his presence caused.

'Not beating right, is it?' Finn said, and she blinked. Was it so obvious?

He sighed at her blank look. 'Mrs Linley. Perhaps she'd better go and see a specialist.'

Mrs Linley. Of course. Janna nodded. 'Finn? Tell her gently. She's a terrible worrier.'

'I will. Any chance of a coffee?'

'Give me five minutes—I've got a dressing to do, then I'm finished and going on my rounds. I'll do it then, before I go out.'

'Thanks. How was the baby?'

She softened. 'Gorgeous. Sleeping peacefully, quite unaware of all the stress she caused us all.'

Finn snorted. 'Typical woman.'

Janna opened her mouth to retaliate, saw Finn's eyes twinkle and shut her mouth again. 'I must say you look very stressed,' she said calmly, and walked out.

Behind her she heard him mutter something about not knowing the half of it, and then the scrape of his chair. 'Mrs Linley, would you come in?' he said, and, smiling reassurance at the woman, Janna crossed the hall to the relative sanctuary of her own room and closed the door.

Mr Gibbs was waiting for a new dressing on his leg where he had cut it on Monday when he fell. It had needed ten stitches and must have interfered quite severely with the walking he had had planned for his holiday. However, he looked quite content for a minute, deep in conversation with old Jamie Barr, so she left him there while she quietly cleared up the mess from the ECG and laid out the dressings pack.

She realised now that she wasn't going to be able to keep Finn at an emotional distance—at least, she wouldn't be able to fool herself, even if she stood the slightest chance of fooling him. She was no longer sure that she could even do that.

Perhaps if she buried herself in her work her sanity might return. With a doubtful snort, she opened her door and called Mr Gibbs in for his dressing.

*   *   *

The rest of the week passed quickly for Janna. She was kept busy, not only by the visitors, with their usual stream of minor injuries and complaints, but by her elderly patients, who seemed just at the moment to be demanding more and more of her time.

Finn had tried Mrs Buchan with sleeping-pills, but they left her more confused during the day, and Finn was worried she would take more than she should by accident, forgetting she had had them.

Janna went to see her again on Friday morning and carefully broached the subject of residential care, only to be met with a blank refusal to discuss the matter. It was as if the old lady hadn't heard what she'd said, Janna thought. She would have to get Finn to have a go—maybe over the weekend, while he was here with his mother and not working. Perhaps he would have more luck.

On the way back, at lunchtime on Friday, she passed old Willy MacPhee, mending a fence near his croft. She pulled over and got out of the car, smiling and waving to him.

'Hello, Willy. How are you and Mrs MacPhee?'

'Oh, keeping well enough, lass. She's been feeling housebound, y'ken, but we'll be oot and aboot now— I've bought mysel' a new car,' he said proudly.

'Really? That's nice.'

'Aye—a brand new one. First I've ever had.'

Janna blinked. She hadn't realised he had that much money, but nothing would surprise her about the secretive old codger.

'Aye,' he went on, 'I sold the barn for a good bit.'

'What?' Janna felt the blood drain from her face. 'Which barn?'

He fastened off the loose wire with a twist of pliers,

then straightened up. 'The one down at Camas Ciuicharan.'

'But, Willy, you knew I wanted to buy it from you!'

He shoved a grubby hand under his cap and scratched his scalp thoughtfully. 'Aye, lass, but what would ye have done wi' it? At least this way it'll be used.'

'But I would have used it—Willy, you *knew*——'

'Ach, well, I'm sorry, lass, but I'd just had a letter from that whining auld goat at the bank, and the offer couldn't have come at a better time. Besides, it was cash. I didnae ha' tae wait for any mortgage to come through.'

'Willy, I had the money sitting in the building society!' she wailed. 'Why didn't you ring me?'

He tutted and shook his head. 'I'm sorry, lass. I didnae ken you were that serious.'

She swallowed her disappointment. 'I suppose the deal's gone through already?' she asked, without any real hope. If he'd bought the car, it must have done.

'Oh, aye, lass—months ago. Young Angus has started work already, I gather.'

Angus Drummond was the local builder, and was kept busy by the demand for new holiday homes in the area. Janna was appalled to think that her barn would be turned into a holiday cottage and would be lost to her forever.

'Oh, Willy—not another holiday cottage? I would have *lived* there——'

'Nae, lass, not a holiday cottage. Finn'll be living there hissel'.'

'Finn?' The sharp stab of betrayal cut Janna to the quick, and she heard her voice rising. 'You sold it to Finn McGregor?'

'Aye—I'm surprised he's nae told you.'

Janna's mouth clamped shut, holding in her anger and disappointment. 'No, Willy, he's not told me. Give my regards to Mrs MacPhee, would you?'

She turned and got back into her car, pulling away and driving off towards her home.

On the way she passed the turning to Camas Ciuicharan and, unbidden, found herself going down the road towards the little bay.

Sure enough, there was the builder's van, pulled up on the grass beside the barn, and sounds of sawing and hammering came from inside the building.

Slowly, her heart torn in two, she walked towards her dream home—now Finn's.

Angus looked up and greeted her with a smile. 'Hello, Janna. Can I help you?'

She shook her head numbly. 'No, Angus, you carry on. I just wondered how you were doing.'

'Slowly but surely. Got to get the doorway and windows shored up and the roof on, then we'll cut away the floor and lay a damp course, and put the floor in, and we're away. The stonework's mainly sound, luckily, so we'll just have to repoint it and tidy it up here and there. Have you seen Finn?'

'No,' she said, her jaws aching from clamping them together to keep the frustration and disappointment inside. 'No, I haven't seen him. I will this afternoon, though.' And God help him, she thought.

'Tell him he'll need to make a decision on the window frames, and I could do with speaking to him about the kitchen units so I can get them under way.'

She nodded. 'I'll tell him.'

She turned and walked back to her car, the urge to cry almost overwhelming her. Damn Finn McGregor!

He had just arrived to do his surgery when she got back to her house.

'Angus Drummond wants to speak to you,' she told him tightly, without looking at him. 'Something about window frames and kitchen units.'

'Oh—right. I'll go and see him after surgery.'

She walked past him into the kitchen, grabbed the bag of bread out of the fridge and savagely buttered a slice. Behind her, Finn was thoughtfully silent.

She seized the peanut butter and spread it on, then folded the bread in half and bit a chunk out.

'Janna?' Finn's voice was soft—cautious.

'Yes?'

'What's wrong?'

'Wrong?' she mumbled round another bite. 'What could possibly be wrong? Everything's simply peachy——'

Her voice cracked and she dropped her head forward, clenching her fists together on the worktop. Damn it, she wouldn't cry—she wouldn't!

Finn's hands on her shoulders were warm and gentle. 'Janna, tell me what's wrong,' he coaxed.

'You,' she whispered harshly. 'Since you came back everything's gone wrong.'

'What now?'

'The barn,' she choked. 'You bought the damn thing—it was mine! I was going to have it—I'd asked MacPhee a million times and he just refused to sell it to me, but you come along, a man, and that's fine, he'll let you have it, and now I'll never have it and I wanted it, and you knew that, or you would have had the courage to tell me you'd bought it!'

'Courage?' he said softly. 'Courage had nothing to do with it. I was leaving it till there was something to look at, then I was going to take you down there and show it to you.'

She spun round, glaring up at him. 'Why? So you could rub it in my face? Damn you, Finn, why did you have to ruin my dream?'

The tears wouldn't be held back any more, and she balled her fists and beat them against his chest. With a soothing murmur he drew her into his arms and folded her against his chest, and her fists, instead of pushing him away, latched on to his shirt like a lifeline, and clung as she wept out her terrible disappointment.

Finally she hiccuped to a halt, and, flattening her hands against his chest, she pushed him away and straightend up.

He tipped her head back with one strong, blunt fingertip. 'Look at me,' he said softly. She opened her aching eyes and his face swam gently into focus. 'I'm sorry you're so angry that I bought the barn. I never meant to hurt you.'

She shook her head. 'It was MacPhee—he knew. He just thought that being a woman I wouldn't do the right thing with it. He trusts you, just like everybody trusts you.' She couldn't keep the bitterness from her voice, and Finn sighed quietly.

'Everybody except you.' He sighed heavily. 'I wish I knew what I'd done to hurt you so badly.'

Janna nearly laughed. What he'd done? How could he be so dense? She pushed away, realising as she did so that her peanut butter sandwich was now squashed into the front of his otherwise immaculate white shirt.

She started to fuss with it, anything to change the subject away from how Finn had hurt her all those years ago. If she started on that now she'd only say something she'd deeply regret, and it would then be impossible to work with him.

So she mopped and blotted and sponged his shirt, trying to ignore the dark curls clearly visible through the fine white cotton, and then she took a towel and rubbed the damp patches briskly, her jaw clenched hard.

Finn stood there and tolerated her less than gentle ministrations, until finally he took the towel out of her furious fingers. 'I think that'll do,' he said calmly, and, hanging it back up, he gave her a steady look.

'You aren't going to talk about it, are you?' he said.

She shook her head. 'No. There's no point, Finn. It was years ago. We have to move on.'

She went out of the kitchen and into her room, replenished her supplies, and then checked that Finn wouldn't need her before going back out to finish her rounds.

The last call of the day was Jessie McGregor, Finn's mother. Janna let herself in, calling as she went, and found Jessie sitting in the living-room with a picture of Finn's father on her lap, her cheeks wet with tears.

'Oh, Janna—I didnae hear you come in, love.' Flustered, she put the picture down and dabbed ineffectually at her wet face.

Janna picked up the photo and looked at it. It showed Finn's father Dougal, standing on board the lifeboat on which he had been a volunteer. A shepherd, he had lived in the modest little croft that was part of Janna's family estate all his married life, scratching a living from the sparse land with sheep and a few head of Highland cattle. It had been a hard life, but simple and honest, and Dougal hadn't minded. He had loved the wild and rugged countryside, and he had taught

Finn all he knew about it, sharing his wide and often intuitive knowledge with the gangly boy who had always been at his side, and with the wide-eyed little girl who had trailed adoringly behind him.

Finn's father had been so like him, big and gentle, a quiet, generous man, whom everyone had admired. He had died six years ago on the lifeboat, trying to rescue a yachtsman who had got into difficulties in a squall. The lifeboat had gone down, taking Finn's father and three other men with it. Their bodies had never been found, and the village had never truly recovered from the tragedy.

Certainly Jessie hadn't. Janna sat beside her and took her hand, squeezing it comfortingly.

'Oh, Janna, I miss him so,' Jessie whispered, and Janna held her as she cried the old, sad tears of her loss. Janna missed him too, as did everyone, but only Jessie had known the real man. Jessie and Finn, perhaps.

Had Finn grieved? She didn't know. She had been busy avoiding him at the time, and she felt a sudden pain that she hadn't been there for him when he'd needed her. Still, she hadn't wanted to intrude, and for the first time she had found herself unable to talk to him.

Had she lost touch with him even then?

She made Jessie a cup of tea and let her talk, then dressed her leg ulcer, noting that it was failing to respond.

The collagen dressings usually worked wonders, but this ulcer was being stubbornly resistant. She smeared a little paste in the deeply pitted centre, to clean the skin back to healthy, living tissue over the next few days. She would see if that worked. Hopefully, it would, and then Jessie would be able to get out and about more. Maybe that would cheer her up a bit and take the edge off her unhappiness.

Just as she was finishing she heard the door open and close, and Finn's light, steady tread behind her.

'Janna, I could do that to save you.'

'I don't mind. Anyway, Finn, you probably wouldn't know where to start,' she teased, winking at Jessie.

He snorted. 'Cup of tea, anyone?'

'We've had one—there's some in the pot,' Janna told him, rolling up the stocking and gathering her things together.

She stood up, bent and kissed Jessie on the cheek and went through to the kitchen.

'She's a bit down, Finn,' she told him quietly. 'She was having a bit of a weep when I arrived.'

'Aye, I could tell. Anything in particular?'

'She had the picture of your father on her lap—the one on the lifeboat.'

Finn nodded. 'She often sits and holds it, I've noticed. Oh, well, I'll have to take her down to see the barn over the weekend.'

Something occurred to Janna. 'Does she realise you won't be living here with her, Finn?' she asked.

He nodded. 'Oh, yes. She thinks the barn's a wonderful idea. She says she'll be able to come and sit by the window and look out over the sea. That's where my father died, in the narrows between the bay and the islands. She feels closer to him when she can see it.'

His voice was gruffer, Janna realised, and, looking up at him, she saw his eyes were bright. 'You still miss him, don't you?' she said softly.

He looked down at her, and she saw Jessie's sadness

mirrored in his blue-grey eyes. 'Aye—aye, Janna, I miss him,' he murmured. 'He was one of my few real friends.'

And she, she realised, had been another.

What had happened to them? She had lost more than her lover that summer seven years ago. She had lost her best and probably her only true friend.

His hand reached out and his thumb brushed her cheek, his touch light as a bird's wing. 'I'm not doing too well, am I? Somewhere along the way I seem to have lost you, as well.'

She swallowed the lump that seemed to be lodged in her throat. 'We've both changed, Finn. It's not so simple any more.'

'Why?' he asked. 'What's so complicated about it? We were friends before—surely we can't have lost all that, Janna?'

She sighed. He wanted to be friends again, to pick up the threads of their friendship, but how could they? There was so much she didn't know about him now, and he about her. The old Finn would have known how much she wanted that barn—could never have bought it without asking her first and, having bought it, would have shared every second of its reconstruction with her.

This Finn standing in front of her was not her childhood friend any more. Fashioned by life, changed by circumstances she had no knowledge of, he had become a stranger to her—a familiar stranger, but a stranger none the less.

'There's so much in the way,' she explained.

'Old water under broken bridges, Janna,' he murmured softly. 'Can't we start again? Forget all our old hurts, put them on one side and get to know each other again from scratch? You're right, we don't know the adults we've become, but the girl I knew can't have changed that much. Please, Janna?' His eyes were searching, staring deep into her soul, and Janna couldn't find the strength to say no.

She'd probably regret it for the rest of her days, but there was a part of her that needed him, defying common sense and reason, and it was a part she couldn't fight any more.

Drawing a steadying breath, she looked up into those beautiful, all-seeing eyes and felt her willpower crumble.

'All right, Finn,' she said softly. 'We'll start again.' And God help us both.

but his eyes said something quite different that made her quiver inside.

'Or chance I put boots on the sand hoping to disguise the government...

CHAPTER FOUR

By Saturday morning Janna was wondering what Finn had done to her willpower. Her decision to keep an emotional distance from him had lasted all of two weeks.

Two whole weeks! On second thoughts, she decided she'd probably done quite well, considering the power of his personality and the sheer strength of his appeal.

And now she was going to expose herself to his wretched appeal again, by going out for a walk with him! It was a beautiful day, the sun blazing down out of a clear blue sky with hardly a cloud to be seen. They were going up the hill behind Camas Ciuicharan, over the headland and down to Port Mackie for lunch, then back again over the rocks while the tide was out.

It was a walk they'd done many times as children, and Janna found herself bubbling over with anticipation as she laced her sturdy walking-boots and waited for Finn's arrival.

She heard the swish of tyres, the steady clatter of a big diesel engine, and then silence, followed by the slam of a car door.

The scrunch of booted feet up to the door coincided with her own footsteps across the hall, and she opened the door just as Finn's hand was raised to knock.

He dropped it slowly to his side, his eyes running down her body to her feet and then flicking back up to her face. 'Good, you put boots on,' his mouth said, but his eyes said something quite different that made her quiver inside.

'Of course I put boots on,' she said lightly, to disguise the quiver. 'Shall we go?'

'Fine. I've got a rucksack with some biscuits and a bottle of drink and my camera. Do you want to put your waterproofs in it?'

She laughed. 'Finn, there's not a cloud in the sky!'

'At the moment. Come on, get them, there's a good girl.'

Grumbling goodnaturedly, she went and fetched them, because she knew he was right. The weather could change in seconds, and the unwary could come to grief. She also brought a sweatshirt, just in case.

She almost ran back to the door, handing them to him with a grin. 'OK now?'

He nodded. 'You look happy.'

She laughed. 'I am. I haven't been out for a walk for ages.'

His smile was wry. 'Nothing to do with the congenial company, then?'

'Of course not,' she said with another laugh, and almost bounced up into the passenger seat of Finn's Discovery.

Finn stowed her waterproofs in his rucksack in the back, then came round and swung himself up behind the wheel, throwing her that cheeky grin she remembered so well. 'All set?'

She nodded.

'Right, let's go.' He started the car, swung off the drive and headed for Camas Ciuicharan. They didn't talk. Janna let her head rest back against the head-restraint and listened to the music Finn put on. It was classical, very soothing, and highly suited to the craggy hills and steep-sided glens they passed through. Every now and then she caught a glimpse of the sea through a gap in the mountains, and as for once she wasn't driving she was able to appreciate the scenery even more.

They passed a little loch, its surface almost completely covered in pinky-white water lilies, and Janna let her breath out in a sigh of sheer delight.

Finn must have heard her. 'Beautiful, isn't it?' he said reverently. 'I can't tell you how much I love it here, or how much I've missed it.'

'You don't need to. I remember while I was away doing my training how much I longed for it. I was only away six years—you've been gone twelve.'

'Aye—and it feels every last day of it,' he said quietly.

He turned down the road to Camas Ciuicharan, winding along the floor of the glen until with a twist the road came out by the side of the bay. He drove the car on to the little track and parked it there alongside the barn—his barn, Janna reminded herself.

He switched off the engine and reached across for her hand. 'Janna?'

She met his eyes. 'Yes?'

'Come and see it—let me tell you what I've got planned.'

The pain was almost tangible, but there was no point crying over spilt milk, and if it had to belong to someone other than her, she would rather it was Finn.

So she got out of the car and followed him inside the barn. It was little more than a shell, perhaps twenty feet wide by thirty-five feet long, but the most important feature for her was the big doorway that opened towards the sea. She had intended to glaze it completely and have that end as the living area, with a bedroom and bathroom at the other end.

Finn's ideas were probably different, though, and she vowed to hold her tongue.

However, he surprised her, although she probably shouldn't have been surprised. Granted, he was putting three bedrooms and a bathroom upstairs, with roof windows, rather than her one downstairs, but his vision for the living area was the same as hers—one large, open room facing the view, with the kitchen opening off it, and only a study and cloakroom at the far end beyond the stairs closed off in the conventional way.

He was going to use natural materials—wood and stone and brick—and have the floor downstairs slate-flagged throughout, with simple wool or cotton scatter-rugs to warm and soften it. The furniture would be simple, he told her: old pine dressers and chests, a sofa and chairs upholstered in plain calico, with scatter-cushions in earth colours of slate and terracotta and pale gold. And the walls would be stone, or plastered and painted white, hung with unframed contemporary oil paintings.

'A friend in Edinburgh did them—fantastic landscapes in wild, wonderful brushstrokes and all the right rich earthy colours—fabulous stuff. I'll show you them one day; they're at my mother's. And upstairs, I thought. . .'

As he talked, Janna found herself picturing it, and him in it, and the pang of longing he evoked in her caused a huge lump in her throat.

He ran on and on, his enthusiasm and obvious excitement doing nothing to soothe her. She wanted nothing more than to share it with him, but even if their new attempt at a relationship seemed to be working, would she ever be able to forget the way he had so easily walked away from her before?

No. Wounds that deep never healed without scarring, and anyway it was a huge leap from 'Let's have another go at being friends' to 'Janna, I love you. I'm sorry I hurt you so callously, will you marry me?'. She sighed, and Finn stopped talking instantly and looked at her, then stabbed his hand through his hair and let out his breath in a gust.

'Hell, Janna, I'm sorry,' he muttered. 'Talk about grinding it in.'

She dredged up a smile. 'Don't worry. It sounds wonderful. I'm glad you're doing it like that, and I'm glad it'll be done properly, not just flung together as a holiday cottage.' She glanced at her watch, then up at the sky. 'If we're going for this walk, had we better go?'

He looked as if he was going to say something else, but then he nodded. 'Sure. We'll go now. I'll get the rucksack.'

For the first few minutes they proceeded in silence, but then the track widened and Finn hung back, waiting for her, his eyes searching her face.

'OK?' he asked. He was still concerned about having hurt her, she knew, but she wasn't ready to talk about it with him. Where Finn was concerned her feelings were all too raw, and so she lied.

'I'm fine,' she said, 'just a bit puffed. I haven't walked uphill for a while.'

She was deliberately changing the subject, and Finn knew that. He took her hand and gave it a little squeeze, then, still holding it, he started walking again, so that she had no option but to fall into step beside him. Not that she minded, exactly. It was just that when she was so close to him, with her hand almost lost in his, she was so much more aware of the power of his beautifully honed body moving easily beside her.

It was distracting enough just being on the same hillside with him. To have this contact with him all the way was almost more than she could cope with.

Finally, however, they reached the top of the headland and he released her hand, turning her so that she could look back over the bay, with the barn nestled at the foot of the glen and the sea like glass stretched out before them all the way to the islands. There was a touch of mist on the sea, drifting in layers, so that the islands seemed to float in mid-air, like something out of a fairytale. In the distance they could hear the chug of a fishing-boat, and far below them the laughter of children playing on the pale, clean sand.

'Isn't it beautiful?' he murmured. 'Of all the places in the world, this has to be the most precious to me. That was why I wanted the barn. It's as if all my friends are gathered here—my father, out there somewhere in the mist, Fergus, Lindsay, you—especially you.'

He turned to her, his voice suddenly softer and slightly husky. 'The barn and you are linked in my mind, Janna. I'm sorry I went on and on, but for some crazy reason it's important to me that I have your approval for my plans. I need you to like what I'm going to do.' He shrugged, as if he didn't understand the need but simply recognised it.

Janna understood. There had been times when she had had to do things she was unsure about, and she had been desperate to have Finn there to talk to about them, to bounce ideas off and rubber-stamp her decisions. No one else would do—none of her colleagues, not her friends, her parents—none of them made an adequate substitute for Finn.

And so she understood his need, and also his reasons for needing to live here, to be close to the father he had loved and lost. And because of that, because she understood, she was able to let go of the last traces of her resentment. She would still regret that the barn wasn't hers, but she had to admit that Finn would do it better. Not simply because he could afford to do it better, but because he also had clearer vision, and so wouldn't muddle the clarity of the design with an unworkable picture bought on impulse and needing a home, or a favourite chair that clashed with the colour scheme.

She smiled gently at him. 'I do like what you're going to do. I think it will be wonderful. I hope you're really happy there.'

The strain around his eyes eased, and a tender half-smile touched his mouth.

'Bless you,' he murmured. His hand came up and cupped her cheek. 'You're very generous. You're also very beautiful.'

She felt the soft blush stain her skin, and then she forgot about it, about everything, because Finn was reaching for her, and the look in his eyes took her breath away.

She closed her eyes so she could breathe, but the suspense was too much and they flickered open again, locking with his as his hands came up and cupped her face, steadying it as his mouth lowered to hers.

The first touch was like the kiss of an angel, light and delicate, his lips firm but gentle, coaxing her response.

Not that she needed coaxing. She had been longing to taste him since Bill MacWhirter's party two weeks ago, and with a shaky sigh her lids fluttered down and she opened her mouth to him.

He tasted the same.

It was her last coherent thought as the soft, moist velvet of his tongue swept her mouth, tracing the line of her teeth, dallying with her tongue and playing tag, drawing it into his mouth and suckling on it until she could have wept.

Her hands slid up over the solid planes of his chest and she found her fingers had threaded through his hair, testing the thick, silky texture as her mouth greedily devoured his.

His arms moved, one hand steadying the back of her head, the other sliding down to cup her bottom and draw her deeper into the cradle of his thighs.

He wanted her. The knowledge shocked and excited her, and with a ragged moan she moved closer, pressing herself to him and revelling in the feel of his hard body against her softer, more yielding form.

Her breasts were crushed against his chest, their softness pillowing the hard muscles and planes of his ribcage. She wanted to touch him, to feel nothing between them but air, to be able to reach out to him and feel the silken texture of his skin, to lie with him and feel his weight. The primitive and elemental need within her was consuming her and driving her wild for him.

She laid a hand against his chest, but all she could feel was the fabric of his T-shirt. With a frustrated moan she tugged at it, and then Finn's hand was on hers, wrapping it in his fingers, stilling its frantic plucking.

'Steady, Janna,' he murmured, his lips warm against her cheek, her ear, her hair. She felt him ease away, felt the loss of contact like a physical pain, and then hard on its heels came a wash of humiliation.

Whatever must he think of her? She dragged herself out of his arms and turned away, her arms wrapping round her waist and hanging on like grim death as wave after wave of shock and pain and need rippled through her.

'Janna?' he said softly.

'I'm all right,' she muttered through tight lips.

'Well, I'm not,' he said, and his voice was wry with humour and taut with something very akin to her own pain.

She turned, hardly daring to look at him, and saw her own feelings reflected in his eyes. He held out his hand and she went back into his arms, standing in their loose embrace, her head pillowed on his chest and her ear against his pounding heart. Gradually it slowed, and she lifted her head reluctantly and met his eyes.

He smiled, his eyes tender and full of wry humour.

'That,' he said slowly, 'was a hell of a kiss.'

She laughed shakily. 'Wasn't it just?'

Carefully, reluctantly, she moved out of his arms again and stood there, unsure what to do next.

Finn made it easy, his gentle humour defusing the situation as only he could. 'As I see it,' he said, staring out over the sea, 'we can stay up here setting fire to the heather, and risk walkers using the coastal path trampling over us on their way, or we can go down into Port Mackie and feed our shattered nerves and try and get a grip on our hormones. Now, I'm very torn, but, as we both have a reputation to protect, I reluctantly vote for the latter.'

He shot her a laughing look. 'Are we going to have

a unanimous vote, or are you going to insist we liven things up for the tourists?'

She giggled. 'Finn, you're impossible. Anyway, I'm hungry.'

He rolled his eyes. 'Well, surprise, surprise. She's hungry. Now, why didn't I guess that?'

She hit him, just lightly, but it was enough, and he reached out to grab her. Laughing, she ran away, darting off down the path to Port Mackie with Finn hollering in hot pursuit.

Years before, in their youth, they had done hill-running together, and the old skills came back to her as she wound her way fast but carefully down the track.

A stone bounced past her, and she could hear Finn's breathing over the pounding of his boots. Suddenly a hand clamped on her shoulder and she shrieked and ducked away, laughter interfering with her breathing as Finn closed on her again, grabbing her round the waist and lifting her off her feet.

He jogged to a halt, his breath coming hard, and she looked over her shoulder into his laughing eyes.

'Witch,' he said. 'You could have killed yourself running like that.' But he was smiling, his eyes alight with exhilaration and mischief, and suddenly he was the old Finn, the boy of her childhood.

He set her down but didn't release her, and she turned in his arms and lifted her hand to cup his jaw.

'Welcome back, Finn,' she said softly.

The laughter left his eyes, replaced by something deeper and closer to his soul. Their eyes still locked, he turned his head and kissed her palm.

'Thank you,' he said softly. Then he stepped back, dropping his arms, and held out a hand to her. 'Lunch?' he suggested.

'Sounds good to me.'

Hand in hand, they made their way down the rest of the hill into Port Mackie.

'Perfect timing,' Finn said as the mobile fish and chip van drove in and parked by the side of the only road.

They bought their lunch and went and sat on a flat rock overlooking the little bay while they ate, and then afterwards Finn stretched out on the rock, as he had many times in the past, and Janna lay down at right angles, with her head pillowed on his stomach, and they dozed in the warm sun while they waited for the tide to go out.

It was a perfect day, the soft suck of the water mingling with the cries of the gulls wheeling overhead, and in the distance Janna could hear the shrieks and giggles of children playing in the chilly water.

If she opened her eyes she would see the rock Finn used to dive off, well above the water even at high tide. Her father and mother had forbidden her to dive from it, but as soon as she had mastered diving at school she had immediately gone up to Finn's rock and dived off.

The tide, unfortunately, had not been at its height, and she had broken a finger hitting the firm sand at the bottom. Finn had been racked with guilt and remorse, and had taken her home in tears to her furious parents.

She hadn't been allowed to swim at Port Mackie for the rest of the holidays, but she had, anyway.

Her mouth tipped in an unconscious smile as she remembered the handful she had been as a child.

'Penny for them,' Finn said, his voice husky.

She turned her head so she was facing him. He was

propped up on one elbow, watching her, and must have seen her smile.

'I was thinking about the time I broke my finger.'

Finn laughed. 'My father threatened to tan me for that.'

She sat up, her eyes opened wide. 'He did what? You were sixteen!'

'Aye—and big enough to know better. Instead of tanning me he sat me down and talked about responsibilities and setting examples and not leading you astray. I don't think anyone had the slightest idea how firmly I kept you in check.' He gave a wry laugh. 'All through my life I was thrashed for things you'd done because I was supposed to have talked you into it.'

Janna was appalled. 'But you never talked me into anything! If it hadn't been for you, I probably would have killed myself a million times in my childhood.'

He lay back down again with a smile. 'That's a nonsensical remark,' he said drowsily. 'How's the tide?'

She swivelled and cast a practised eye over the rocks on the other side of the bay. 'Right out. It might even have just turned.'

'Shall we go?'

'Mmm.' She rose to her feet and gave him a hand up, just to touch him, and then found herself watching him as he shrugged into the rucksack, the muscles of his shoulders rippling under the T-shirt.

She looked away quickly. What was wrong with her? It was that wretched kiss, of course, stirring everything up again and leaving her aching for more.

'All set?' he asked.

She nodded and, turning, set off across the rocks towards Camas Ciuicharan. Finn followed a few steps behind her as she picked her way between the masses of black seaweed, treading where possible on the rough little barnacles that gave some grip.

The rockpools were wonderful, teeming with life, and they paused every now and again to study them. A young plaice was trapped in one, its dark speckled skin blending so well with the rock that they could hardly see it. Only Finn's sharp eyes picked it out. Janna was too busy trying not to look at his hand as he pointed to things.

As they rounded the headland they could hear a child crying. 'Oh, dear,' Finn murmured. 'Someone's not very happy.'

'Probably cut herself,' Janna said. 'Do we go and see, or leave it to the parents?'

He shrugged. 'You know kids—I expect her big brother poked her sea anemone and made it close up!'

Janna shook her head. 'She sounds frightened, Finn.'

He listened, his head tipped on one side, and then nodded. 'I think you're right. We'd better check it out, just for our peace of mind.'

They headed over the rocks towards the noise, and then they saw the children, three of them, down on the edge of the water. One, a little girl, was partly in the water, and most of the noise seemed to be coming from her. However, a larger boy, possibly her brother, was tugging at her and yelling.

'You must be able to,' he was shouting.

'But I can't!' she screamed, hysterical now. 'It's stuck!'

'Oops,' Finn said softly. 'I think she's got her foot stuck. Shall we go and investigate before he yanks her leg off?'

'Good idea,' Janna agreed.

Neither of them had the slightest idea what lay

ahead, but they were to be glad later that they had gone to help, because, without them, there might have been a very different outcome, one that would have been very hard to live with.

Finn reached them first, crouching down beside the little group and touching the boy on the shoulder.

'What's the problem, laddie?' he asked quietly.

'Sophie's foot's stuck—she fell off this rock and slid in the water—and now she can't get it out. Stupid girl.'

'I'm not stupid!' the little girl sobbed.

'No, you're not,' Finn agreed, sending the boy a warning look. 'Now, just calm down, Sophie, and we'll try and sort you out. I'm a doctor, and this lady's a nurse. We'll have you out of there in no time.'

Instantly the child quietened, either because of Finn's profession or his gentle, steady voice— or a combination of the two. Whatever, some of the terror left her wide blue eyes and she seemed reassured, happy to hand over her fright to an adult. So was her older brother, who was clearly worried to death.

'Mum'll kill me. I was supposed to be looking after her,' he mumbled.

'Where are your parents?' Janna asked, eyeing the boy. He must have been all of nine, and the other child, another boy, playing happily in a rockpool, was four at the most.

'At the cottage,' the boy told her.

'Mrs Cameron's?'

He nodded. 'I think so—we only got here at lunch-time, but I think it was Mrs Cameron.'

Finn slid the pack off his back, stripped off his T-shirt and lay down on the rocks, his arm up to the elbow in water, feeling around the child's foot.

'What's that?' she screamed. 'It's a crab, I know it is!'

'It's my hand, sweetheart,' Finn assured her, clamping his other hand on her leg to stop her frantic tugging. 'I just want to see how you've managed to get this foot stuck here.'

He groped around for a minute, then withdrew his gripping arm and looked at Janna.

'Her shoe's still on. If we undo the laces she might be able to pull her little foot out of the crack.'

But her foot was turned sideways, and after some time Finn muttered something under his breath.

'Problems?' Janna asked.

He nodded. 'The lace has knotted. I'll need to cut the shoe off. Janna, could you and this young man go and find their parents and tell them what's happened? You'd better take the wee lad with you, and bring back some scissors and a sharp kitchen knife.'

'You aren't going to cut my foot off!' the little girl screamed.

Finn wrapped his arms round her and rocked her against his chest reassuringly. 'Shh, sweetheart, nobody's going to cut your foot off. I want to cut your shoe so your foot can come out. Oh, and Janna, could you call Dougie?'

Dougie was the coastguard, and the fact that Finn felt he needed him worried Janna more than anything else could have done.

Taking the little boy's hand, she led him across the rocks, following his big brother. He was slowing her down, however, so, scooping him up on to one hip, she carried him the rest of the way, arriving at the cottage just as the children's parents came out with the older boy.

'Rory tells us Sophie's stuck on a rock,' the father said.

He looked unconcerned, and Janna realised that the full significance of the problem hadn't dawned on them yet—either that or they hadn't understood Rory's panicked explanation.

She was sure it would all become painfully clear all too soon. Not wishing to panic them unnecessarily, she asked them to find the scissors and sharp knife while she ran next door to Mrs Cameron.

'Could I use your phone to call Dougie?' she asked. 'The wee lass next door has got her foot stuck in the rocks down at low tide. Finn's trying to get her out, but we haven't got all that long, the tide's turned already.'

'Oh, my lord!' the woman said, clapping her hands to her cheeks. 'You go, lass. I'll phone Dougie, and I'll wait here for him and send him on. Whereabouts is she?'

Janna gave quick directions and ran back out.

The family were all assembled again, and the mother held out the things she had asked for. 'Are these all right?' she asked.

'Fine,' Janna said. The knife was short-handled, the scissors blunt-ended. At least they wouldn't cut her. 'Have you any Vaseline or that sort of thing?'

'In the car,' the man said. 'I keep some in the toolkit. It's not very clean, but will it do?'

'Wonderful,' Janna said.

He found it in seconds, just as Mrs Cameron came out. 'Leave the children with me,' she told the couple. 'You can do without them to worry about as well.'

Gratefully they handed them over, and then the three adults set off across the rocks, Janna leading.

By the time they arrived back Janna fully expected

Finn to have extracted the child, but to her horror he was still working on her shoelace, and the water level had already risen several inches. She could tell because now, when he put his hand down to Sophie's foot, his chin grazed the water.

As they reached them Sophie's mother crouched down and put her arms round the little girl, and she promptly burst into noisy tears.

The father looked at Finn. 'We've brought the scissors and knife, and some Vaseline.'

Finn nodded. 'I'll try cutting the laces. I don't suppose anyone's got a waterproof torch?'

They shook their heads.

'I'll go,' Janna volunteered, and, after running back over the rocks again, she found Mrs Cameron and Mrs Grainger talking on the beach while the two boys played in the sand a little way away.

'I need a waterproof torch,' she explained breathlessly.

'I'm sure Michael's got one in the boat—hang on,' Mrs Grainger said, and moments later she returned with it.

'Will this do?'

'Perfect,' Janna said, almost grabbing it.

Mrs Grainger handed her a bundle of black neoprene. 'Here—Michael's wet suit. Get Finn to put it on—he's a bit bigger, but it'll save him getting so chilled. And there's a smaller one there you might be able to use for the child.'

With muttered thanks Janna took the things and ran back, grateful for her surefootedness over the rocks but still being very careful. The last thing they needed was a member of the rescue committee getting stuck as well!

Finn greeted the wet suit with a nod. He was already stripped down to his briefs and was squatting in the water, working on Sophie's foot. 'Give me the torch. Let me see if I can get the scissors on this lace before we worry about putting on the wet suit,' he said.

But he couldn't hold the torch and manipulate the scissors, so Janna lay down and held the torch under the water while Finn immersed his head and struggled with the shoe.

When Janna was sure he must have drowned, he lifted his head clear, took several deep breaths and went back under.

The shoe finally gave way to the scissors, and, using the Vaseline, Finn smeared it liberally over Sophie's foot and began trying to work it free.

'Ow—ow, that hurts!' she screamed, but Finn couldn't hear her with his head under water. He must have felt her distress, though, because when he came up for air he looked at Janna and shook his head. 'It'll only come so far, and it's hurting her too much. I don't want to make it swell so we can't get it out in a hurry if we have to, so I've pushed the foot back into the shoe where it's more comfortable. We'll get Dougie to try and break off the bit of rock sticking out just above that's trapping it.'

'But the tide's coming in!' Sophie's mother whispered in a frantic undertone. The urgency of her daughter's situation had obviously dawned on her now, and Janna felt a surge of compassion. She must be absolutely terrified.

'It's only coming in slowly,' Finn lied. 'We've plenty of time. Let's get the wet suit on her to keep her warmer.'

It was a two-piece suit, and they managed to get

one leg and all of the top and arms on to her. Although it was vast on her, by rolling up the cuffs they were able to make it tight enough to keep out some of the water and it certainly kept the wind off. Janna gave their waterproofs to Sophie's parents, and pulled on the sweatshirt she had also included at the last minute. It wouldn't help if it got wet but it might keep the wind off her a bit. Typically of weather in the Highlands, it was beginning to deteriorate without warning.

Finn struggled into Michael's wet suit and slipped back into the chilly water. The zip would only pull up to halfway up his chest, and Janna was worried about him getting too cold if he was in there long. Still, it was better than nothing, and hopefully Dougie would be there soon.

'I'll see if I can find a crack in the rock, any kind of weakness that Dougie can work on,' he said, and Janna watched helplessly as he took the torch from her and worked his way inch by inch over the rock, by now nearly two feet under water.

The tug of the waves was beginning to sway Sophie, so Janna sat on one side of her and her father sat on the other, and her mother perched on the rock in front of her and held her frozen little hands and talked calmingly to her. She seemed to have buried her panic and was distracting Sophie beautifully. Janna wished she was as distracted. All she could see was the rising water, and the tiny girl being gradually swamped while they all stood by helplessly.

After what seemed like an age Dougie arrived, running over the rocks, and Finn came out of the water and led him to one side to fill him in.

Janna could feel the water rising, the rhythmic surge of the swell as the sea reminded them of its awesome power. The child's foot had gone *into* the gap, she reasoned. Surely it would come *out*?

Dougie and Finn approached them, and Dougie smiled reassuringly, but Janna could see that he was concerned.

'I've got an air-powered chisel in the van,' he told them. 'We're going to bring the compressor and all the gear round in Michael Grainger's boat.'

Janna nodded, and watched as Dougie and Finn disappeared over the rocks. It seemed ages as she supported the child against the swell of the incoming tide, before they heard the steady throb of Michael's engine.

Please, God, let them be in time, Janna prayed.

Beside her the little girl was shuddering with cold, and her lips were turning blue. Janna squeezed her shoulder. 'Soon have you out now, sweetheart,' she murmured.

As she turned back towards Finn and Dougie, the wake of the small boat splashed against the rocks and broke over Sophie's head. The tide was coming in fast, and Janna was terribly afraid that help would come too late.

CHAPTER FIVE

SOPHIE was sobbing with terror, her face streaming with water, hair plastered down against her little head. Her eyes in that pale, petrified little face seemed enormous, and Janna's arms ached to be able to sweep her up and carry her away. Instead she wiped the water from her face, cupped the frigid little cheeks in her hands and met her eyes with all the confidence she could muster.

'You see that boat, Sophie? They've brought a special tool that can cut away the rock and let your foot out. I'm going to go and help them get it ready, then I'll come back again, OK?'

Sophie nodded, turning to her parents again as Janna eased herself away from Sophie's side. She stood up awkwardly, her limbs cramped from the seeping cold of the water, and went to help Finn and Dougie tie up the boat and unload the equipment. As soon as she was out of Sophie's earshot, she told Finn her fears.

'I don't want to panic you, but it's getting critical,' she warned.

His gaze locked with hers, and she could see her worries reflected in his eyes. 'I know. We've brought some aqualungs—if the worst comes to the worst, she'll have to breathe through a mask.'

'But she'll be terrified!' Janna protested.

'Not as terrified as if we let her drown—and there's no alternative. Even if I had the necessary equipment, which I don't, there isn't room to amputate her foot. As long as we can keep her going without risking serious hypothermia, we'll do so.'

'And what then, Finn?' she asked.

His eyes closed. 'God knows,' he said bleakly. 'I dare say we'll think of something. We've called Air Sea Rescue—perhaps they've got a spare miracle. Failing that, I'll pull the damn foot out anyway, before I let her drown or freeze to death. Right, Dougie, where do you want the compressor?'

Janna shuddered. She hoped to God it wouldn't come to that, but the situation was looking increasingly desperate. Perhaps the air-chisel would work, if they could get the equipment close enough. However, even that was difficult, because all the surrounding rocks were now if not underwater at least being lapped by the deceptively gentle waves.

Dougie looked around, then shrugged. 'We'll have to leave it in the boat—the pipes are long enough. I'll show you how to work it, then get the boat as close as I can while you work, OK?'

Janna went back to Sophie and her parents and explained what they were going to do as Dougie manoeuvred the boat into position. Once again Finn went back under the water with the torch, then, shrugging into the aqualung and putting the mask over his face, he took the chisel under and left Janna with the job of holding Sophie's other leg out of the way and holding the torch steady, while he used the air-powered chisel on the projecting piece of rock.

Another wave broke over Sophie's head, and Janna tapped Finn on the shoulder. He lifted his head, took one look at Sophie's streaming, shuddering little face and turned to her father.

'She needs the air,' he said. 'Go and get the

spare set from over there, and I'll show her how it works.'

The man lugged the heavy equipment over and Finn gave the terrified little girl a hasty lesson in breathing through the mask. Once she had grasped the essentials, he went quickly back under the water.

Janna could feel the vibration of the chisel through the rock, but Finn didn't seem to be making a great deal of progress. The rock was hard, the position inaccessible, and Sophie's little leg was partly in the way.

In all, it was almost impossible, Janna thought. Just when she was getting ready to panic properly she felt a jolt, Sophie cried out and Finn lifted his head.

Water streaming off his head, he passed her the heavy chisel, signalled to Dougie to turn off the compressor and went back under the water.

'You'll soon be out, darling,' Sophie's father said, but he didn't sound very sure, and Janna could feel the tension in him like steel cables reaching breaking strain.

Finn was working on Sophie's foot, and whatever he was doing obviously hurt because the poor little thing whimpered and then screamed, just as her foot was freed and Finn lifted her clear of the waves.

Sobbing, blood trickling from the scrapes on her swollen and bruised little foot, Sophie clung to her mother and father, all of them weeping openly with relief as Janna gently disentangled the little girl from the aqualung.

Just then Finn lifted his head and gave Janna a weary grin. 'Here come the cavalry,' he mumbled, and in the distance she caught the wop-wop-wop of the Air Sea

Rescue helicopter. It flew down low over them, lowered a man on a winch to the rocks and then went off, on his instructions to Port Mackie, to touch down on the firm sand of the beach.

The winchman approached the little group, assessed the smiles and turned to Finn.

'Are you the chap that got her out?'

Finn nodded wearily. 'Aye. In the end I had to tug a bit, and I could have broken or dislocated one of her tarsal bones on the instep. But there was no other way to get her out.'

The man nodded. 'Well, she looks alive, anyway. We'll check her over and take her to Fort William for observation. How long was she in the water?'

Janna glanced at her watch and realised it had stopped. Finn's, however, was built for that sort of abuse, and Janna was stunned to learn that it was after four. They had been working on the rescue for more than two hours, and for a large part of it they had been in the water. Finn had the wet suit on, with the zip up the front which wouldn't do up all the way, and she realised that Finn was thoroughly chilled. She was, too, and the deep shudders that were running through her made her realise how perilously close they all were to hypothermia. Finn had been wet the longest, though. She turned to him.

'Are you OK?' she asked him gently. 'You must be freezing.'

He eyed her searchingly. 'I'm all right—I'm cold, but I'm OK. You weren't nearly as well-protected. We'll see them off, then go back to your place and warm up, and I'll check you over. I don't think there's much wrong with either of us that some hot cocoa and a warm room won't cure.'

It sounded wonderful, Janna hadn't realised how cold she was until they arrived back at Port Mackie and Mrs Cameron wrapped her cardigan round Janna's shoulders and put a cup of steaming, homemade broth in her hand. 'Here, you're frozen half to death. Drink this,' she told them all, and they did, curling their stiff fingers round the cups and sipping cautiously. Janna could feel the soup warming her as she swallowed it, and she clung to the mug, trying not to slop the contents as the shudders ran through her.

Finn tapped her on the shoulder. 'Sophie's OK,' he told her. 'Her foot's mangled but I don't seem to have damaged it too much. I think she's cold and shocked as much as anything.'

Janna nodded. That seemed entirely likely. It had been a horrendous ordeal for the poor little scrap, and she had been very lucky that the outcome had been so fortunate.

They bundled Sophie up in reflective blankets to keep the warmth in and loaded her into the helicopter, together with her mother. Mrs Cameron promised to warm Sophie's father up and then send him off to Fort William to bring them home once Sophie had been seen and checked over. Because of the wet suit it seemed unlikely that they would need to keep her overnight, but it was possible. The boys, in the meantime, would be spoilt rotten by Mrs Cameron, Janna had no doubt.

'She's a kindly soul,' she said to Finn as they watched her fussing over the remains of the family after the helicopter had gone.

'Aye, she is—maybe now she's even forgiven us for wrecking her garden on the bike.'

Janna laughed. 'Maybe.' A deep shudder ran

through her, and Finn put his arm round her and pulled
her close.

'You're frozen. Dougie, the car's at Camas
Ciuicharan. You couldn't run us back to the Nurse's
House at Kilbarchan, could you? I want to get Janna
into some dry clothes and warmed up a bit. We can
get the car later.'

'Aye, it's on my way,' Dougie said. 'There's only
two seats, but I dare say you can manage Janna on
your lap for that wee distance.'

So they squeezed into Dougie's van, Finn still in
Michael Grainger's wet suit and Janna in her sodden
jeans and T-shirt with Mrs Cameron's cardigan slung
round her. Janna laid her head on Finn's shoulder and
thought how wonderful it felt to be so close to him.
If only she weren't frozen half to death, and her teeth
weren't chattering fit to shatter, it would be quite cosy,
she mused.

They arrived back at the house, let themselves in
and went straight to the bathroom. Modesty forgotten,
Finn stripped off the too-small wet suit and then turned
to Janna. Her fingers were too cold and uncooperative
to undo her soaking jeans, and he quickly released the
stud, slid the zip down and tugged the stiff, sodden
material down her legs.

'God, woman, you're purple and orange with cold,'
he scolded gently. 'Here, let's wrap you in a towel and
get you warmed up.'

Apparently oblivious to her nakedness, he retrieved
some fresh, warm towels from the airing cupboard and
wrapped one sarong-style round her, tucking it in
firmly over her breasts, then draped another round
her shoulders. He did the same himself, then turned
back to her.

'That's better,' he said. 'Now, we could do with putting on something else and having a hot drink. Got any warm, long socks?'

Janna shook her head doubtfully. 'Maybe some slouch socks?'

He nodded. 'Where are they?'

'They're in the bedroom,' she told him. After walking across the landing to her room, she stared blankly at the chest of drawers. Where did she keep her socks? She pressed her hand to her head. Everything felt like cotton wool, and she sat down heavily on the end of the bed.

'I'm sleepy,' she mumbled.

Somewhere in the distance she heard Finn swear, then he was yanking drawers open and pulling out socks and tugging them none too gently over her cold, sticky feet.

Then suddenly she was in his arms and he was carrying her downstairs to the sitting-room. He deposited her on the sofa, threw a rug over her legs and turned on the electric fan heater full blast.

She lay back against the arm of the sofa, her mind like gluey porridge, and listened to the hum of the heater and Finn working in the kitchen. Why was he doing that? She wanted him here.

She tried to call him, but she was too tired to make her mouth work. Instead she lay there, not even shivering any more, and when, moments later, he came back she was almost asleep.

'Janna?'

'Mmm,' she grunted, too sleepy to answer properly.

'Janna, wake up. I want you to have a warm drink, then I need to measure the temperature of your urine.'

She cracked open an eye and inspected him. 'Pervert,' she mumbled.

He swore, softly but comprehensively, and then hauled her up into a sitting position. 'Drink this,' he ordered, and pressed a cup into her hand.

It was hot—not so hot that she couldn't drink it, but satisfyingly warm and sickly sweet. She stared at it for ages. 'Cocoa,' she said eventually, pleased with herself for having identified it at last.

'That's right—drink up.'

She did so, and then he wheeled her into the cloakroom, put a paper bedpan into the top of the loo and pushed her down on it. 'You've got two minutes,' he told her. 'If you don't co-operate I'll take your temperature rectally.'

'Bully,' she mumbled, but she must have performed to his satisfaction because a little while later she was tucked up on the sofa again without any further indignities and he'd disappeared.

A few moments later he came back into the room. 'I knew you should have gone to Fort William,' he growled. He sounded cross with her, and she felt tears welling in her eyes. She was too cold and tired to fight with him.

'Don't shout at me,' she whispered, and then he tugged her to her feet, stripped off all their towels and lay down on the sofa, pulling her down after him and folding her into the curve of his body—his warm, hard, wonderfully comforting and absolutely naked body.

'I said you were a pervert,' she mumbled, and then she gave herself up to the warmth radiating from him and from the light, soft rug he threw over them.

'Go to sleep,' he told her, his voice gruff and comforting in her ear. And, wriggling even closer to that blissful warmth, she felt herself drift away. . .

Janna slowly became aware of two things. One, she was suffocatingly hot, and two, she was wedged against Finn's absolutely naked body—correction, Finn's absolutely naked and distinctly aroused body.

He was fast asleep, his hand curled protectively over one breast, and as she shifted his fingers tightened possessively.

Lifting his hand away, she reached out for the fan heater, but her arm wasn't long enough. She stretched further, and Finn's arm round her waist tightened.

'What are you doing?' he asked sleepily.

'Trying to reach the fire before we suffocate.'

He pulled her back and, lifting himself up, he sprawled across her and stretched out one hugely long arm to flick the switch. As he slid back over her, her breath caught in her throat.

So many sensations! The soft scrape of his body hair over her delicate skin, the feel of smooth, well-honed muscle rippling with the slight effort, the hard, angular jut of his ribcage above the washboard stomach—and, lower, the satin-steel evidence of his arousal, pressed hard against her tender flesh.

They were lying face to face, their eyes locked, and Janna couldn't help herself. Her hands came up and cupped his cheeks. 'Finn, kiss me,' she whispered raggedly.

For an age he was still, then with a shattered groan Finn lowered his head and took her mouth.

This kiss was nothing like an angel's. It was greedy and demanding, and she gave everything he asked and took more; her hands feverishly explored the hot, dry planes of his back, aware of the moment when the fine sheen of sweat broke out across the skin. One hand, possessive, needy, slid down and cupped the hard curve of his buttocks. Unbelievingly she felt the muscles tense even more, and then he began to move against her, rocking gently, making her ache deep down inside.

She shifted against him, her legs trapped, and a moan rose in her throat as she tried to move to accommodate him. He parted his legs and pressed one knee between hers, rocking against her and chafing gently against the soft cushion of her womanhood.

She gasped, the sound swallowed by his mouth, and then his hand came up, easing over her ribs, closing possessively over one breast and kneading the aching peak until she whimpered.

He lifted his head slightly, his mouth hot and greedy, laying a trail of fire down over her jaw and throat, pausing at the hollow to torment the thrashing pulse with the tip of his wicked, skilful tongue, then moving on down, teasing her, until at last he drew her nipple into his hot, hungry mouth.

She sobbed aloud, aching for him, and his hand moved on, tracing the line of her ribs, the smooth swell of her hip, the tender skin of her inner thigh, until at last it closed over the clamouring ache within her.

She bucked beneath him, her reserve swept away by need, and, raising his lips to hers again, he matched the rhythm of his tongue to his hand, stroking her softly with gentle, knowing fingers until the tension exploded, ripping through her in wave after wave of wonderful, glorious release. He swallowed her cries, cradling her against his chest and murmuring softly, until the aftershocks receded and she was still.

Then he eased away from her, his body still taut with unreleased passion, and she lay there, washed with a curious mixture of blissful lassitude and maidenly modesty, and watched him, wondering what he would do next.

'I'm a shameless hussy,' she said with a little catch in her voice.

He sat up, moved to the end of the sofa, his face reflecting a welter of emotions, and covered her again with the rug, tucking it tenderly round her shoulders.

'No,' he murmured. 'You're beautiful. I should be shot for taking advantage of you when you're ill. You deserve better than that.'

She realised he was serious, that he had distanced himself from her and didn't intend to go any further. 'Finn?' she whispered. 'Finn, please, you can't stop— I need you.'

He shook his head, his eyes dark as coals now, brittle with longing. She could see his chest heaving, the need in him still strong—as strong as hers.

'Janna, for God's sake stop looking at me like that,' he groaned, burying his head in his hands, and then he jerked to his feet, snatching up one of their discarded towels and tying it firmly round his waist.

'I'm going to take a shower,' he flung over his shoulder, and, closing the door firmly behind him, he left her alone with her tumbling emotions, not least of which was embarrassment.

It was one thing to make love and feel all those sensations together, she thought in humiliation. It was quite another to do what he had done to her and then walk away. It had left her feeling so—cheap? No. No, the look in his eyes had made her feel anything but.

HOW TO PLAY
SIX HUNDRED THOUSAND
BIG BUCKS
SIX HUNDRED THOUSAND
AND YOU COULD WIN THE
£600,000
PLUS JACKPOT!
YOUR *PERSONAL* GAME CARD INSIDE...
Mills & Boon

THE £600,000 PLUS JACKPOT!

IT'S FUN! IT'S FREE!

BIG BUCKS

It's so easy... grab a coin, and go right to your BIG BUCKS game card. Scratch off silver squares in a STRAIGHT LINE (across, down, or diagonal) until 5 pound signs are revealed. BINGO!.... Doing this makes you eligible for a chance to win £600,000 in lifetime income (£20,000 each year for 30 years)! Also scratch all 4 corners to reveal the pound signs. This entitles you to a chance to win the £30,000 Extra Bonus Prize! Void if more than 9 squares scratched off.

Your EXCLUSIVE PRIZE NUMBER is in the upper right corner of your game card. Return your game card and we'll activate your unique Prize Draw Number, so it's important that your name and address section is completed correctly. This will permit us to identify you and match you with any cash prize rightfully yours!

FREE BOOKS PLUS FREE GIFT!

At the same time you play your BIG BUCKS game card for BIG CASH PRIZES.... scratch the Lucky Charm to receive FOUR FREE Love on Call novels, and a FREE GIFT, TOO! They're totally free, absolutely free with no obligation to buy anything!

These books have a cover price of £1.99 each. But THEY ARE TOTALLY FREE; even the postage and packing will be at our

expense! The Reader Service is not like some book clubs. You don't have to make any minimum number of purchases - not even one!

The fact is, thousands of readers look forward to receiving four of the best new romance novels, at least a month before they're available in the shops. They like the convenience of home delivery, and there is no extra charge for postage and packing.

Of course you may play BIG BUCKS for cash prizes alone by not scratching off your LUCKY CHARM, but why not get everything that we are offering and that you are entitled to? You'll be glad you did!

NO PURCHASE NECESSARY - MILLION DOLLAR SWEEPSTAKES (III)

THE READER SERVICE: HERE'S HOW IT WORKS

Accepting free books places you under no obligation to buy anything. You may keep the books and gift and return the invoice marked "cancel". If we don't hear from you, about a month later we will send you 4 additional books and invoice you for just £1.99* each. That's the complete price, there is no extra charge for postage and packing. You may cancel at any time, otherwise every month we'll send you 4 more books, which you may either purchase or return - the choice is yours.

* Prices and terms subject to change without notice.

Mills & Boon Reader Service

FREEPOST

P.O. Box 70

Croydon

Surrey

CR9 9EL

NO
STAMP
NEEDED

it to:- "Big Bucks" Prize Draw, Harlequin Mills & Boon, P.O. Box 70, Croydon, Surrey CR9 3JE - we'll assign a Prize Draw number to you. Limit - one entry per envelope.

Cheated, then. Selfish. Incomplete. Her breath caught on a sob. Why had he stopped? Didn't he want to make love to her?

Yes, of course he did. Heavens, how much more obvious could it have been? So why stop there? God knew, she'd been willing enough. Too willing, perhaps. Maybe his body was just reacting automatically, as it had in his sleep, and she had come on to him like a sex-starved adolescent—except the last time she had done that he had been more than willing.

So why stop now?

Because he had changed, grown up, matured, and she was no longer his type—if she ever really had been.

What other answer was there?

None. A wave of humiliation washed over her, flooding her skin with soft colour. Why had she behaved like that? She must have been crazy if she couldn't tell he was reluctant. Had he been reluctant before, on her birthday? Perhaps he had just been a young man in the grip of his hormones, without the self-control to deny himself what his body had wanted, even if his mind had known it was a mistake.

And she was sure he thought it was a mistake now. He wanted to be friends, for God's sake! Friends, not lovers, and she'd gone and spoilt it by kissing him like that, and trying to persuade him into something he wasn't ready for and didn't want.

She wanted to die. How could she have been so blind, so totally clueless? Wrapping the rug firmly round her naked body, she went up to her bedroom, locked the door, and dressed quickly in a shapeless tracksuit and sloppy socks. It was about as sexless as she could make herself, and, after brushing her hair without looking at herself, because she found she couldn't meet her eyes in the mirror, she went down to the kitchen.

Finn was putting the kettle on, dressed again in his jeans and T-shirt, his bare feet sticking out and making him look thoroughly at home. Janna suddenly didn't want him looking at home in her house, not after what had happened—or hadn't happened.

'Tea or coffee?' he asked.

Neither, she thought. I just want you out so I can think. 'We ought to go and collect your car,' she said, as casually as she could manage. 'You don't want to leave it there overnight.'

He studied her silently for a moment. She wished she could see the expression on his face, but she didn't dare to look. She just knew he was watching her. She could see him out of the corner of her eye, and she would have given anything other than the tattered remnants of her pride to know what he was thinking.

Just when she thought she was going to scream the doorbell rang, and she almost ran across the hall to answer it. When she opened it she wished she hadn't, because there on the doorstep were her mother and father, obviously dressed to go out to dinner, and there she was in a baggy old sweatsuit and Finn behind her in bare feet!

'Darling!' her mother cried, launching herself over the step and hugging her daughter affectionately. 'Are you all right? We heard what happened and came straight over.' She held Janna at arm's length, studying her face for any clues, and then hugged her again. 'You're all flushed. Shouldn't you be in bed, darling?'

Janna felt her cheeks heat even more. 'I'm fine, Mum,' she said. 'I've had a rest. Finn's been taking care of me.'

She felt the blush deepen and turned to her father, kissing him lightly on the cheek before turning back to the kitchen. 'Finn's still here, actually. He's just put the kettle on. Come on into the kitchen.'

'Well, we mustn't stop long,' Mrs Murray said. 'We're supposed to be at the Jamiesons'—they're having a party. We said we'd be a little late, but we mustn't be too long.'

'Just a cup of tea,' Janna persuaded, suddenly terribly glad that they were here and would fill the silence between her and Finn until she could get rid of him.

She went back into the kitchen, complete with her elegant bodyguard, and found Finn pouring tea into four mugs.

'So, young man, the hero of the hour,' Janna's father said jovially.

Finn laughed. 'I'd forgotten how rapidly news travels in the backwoods. It's good to see you again.'

He shook their hands, confident and comfortable with them as Janna had never seen him. No longer an awkward adolescent or diffident young man, he seemed completely at ease, and Janna's mother, in particular, was charmed by him.

Janna, on the other hand, just wanted him out of the house as rapidly as possible before she died of embarrassment. However, she was to be thwarted.

'Why don't we go through to the sitting-room?' her mother suggested.

Janna's eyes widened. The sitting-room was in chaos! There were towels strewn across the floor, the cushions were piled up at one end of the settee and she was sure the air was still painted red with passion.

She opened her mouth to protest that it was comfortable in the kitchen but she was too slow. Her mother had gone, closely followed by her father and Finn.

Trailing, she waited for the gasps and comments, but none came. Once she was in there she saw why. The towels were gone, the cushions plumped up and redistributed, and the passion-painted air had been evicted via the open window. Her shoulders must have drooped with relief, because Finn shot her a knowing smile for which she could cheerfully have killed him.

Her parents took the two chairs, her mother saying as they sat down, 'Are you all right there, Finn? Would you rather have the chair? I'd forgotten how big you are now.'

He laughed, settling into one end of the sofa. 'We're fine, Mrs Murray. Janna and I fit quite comfortably together on here.'

Janna felt her cheeks heat again and bent her head, so that her hair fell forward and concealed the blush from her mother's all too sharp eyes. Focusing on her tea, she let Finn carry the conversation. If he wanted to charm them, let him.

He did. Janna found herself drifting in and out of a light doze as Finn related the events of the day— the abridged version, she thought. The most traumatic part of the day as far as Janna was concerned was too hot to handle in conversation. She could just imagine Finn explaining it. 'Oh, and after all that your daughter tried to seduce me, but I resisted.'

She felt herself relax as they moved away from the subject of the rescue. Somehow she couldn't find the energy to be angry with Finn any more for what he had done. The strain of the day, the physical toll of hypothermia and then the emotional rollercoaster of Finn's lovemaking had left her exhausted, and she rested her head against the wing of the sofa and let them all get on with it.

'Darling, we should be thinking about going if we're going to get to the Jamiesons' tonight—we're already late,' Janna's mother said.

Her reprieve was over. How could she get rid of Finn? She really couldn't cope with being here alone with him. She roused herself to see them off, her mind desperately groping for a reason to send him on his way, but he saved her the effort. As they were standing in the hall, Finn eyed her and then turned to her father.

'Mr Murray, I don't know if you'd have time to run me down to Camas Ciuicharan on your way to the Jamiesons'? We left the car there this morning. Janna and I were going out to get it now, but she looks out on her feet. I think she should get to bed; she's had a difficult day.'

'Difficult' wasn't the way Janna would have described it, but she couldn't argue, not there in front of her parents. Finn pulled on his soggy boots, picked up his rucksack and then confounded Janna by dropping a kiss on her cheek. 'Get to bed, love. You look shattered.'

Not surprisingly, she thought. Then her mother totally wrecked what was left of her peace of mind, just when she thought they were leaving and things were getting better.

'Finn, why don't you bring your mother over for lunch tomorrow? We've got a haunch of venison and it seems wicked not to share it. You'd both be more than welcome. Nothing formal—we always have Sunday lunch in the kitchen, because our cook has the day off and I can't be bothered to walk miles just to lay the table! It seems such a waste of effort, but Mrs

Smith likes to do it properly. Personally, we prefer the kitchen, but I haven't got the nerve to tell her.'

Finn's smile was wry. 'Thank you, I'll look forward to it, and I'm sure my mother will too.'

'Good—about twelve to twelve-thirty? Janna will be there, won't you, darling?'

'I will?' she said dumbly.

'Yes—you remember, I asked you a week or so ago and you said you could because you weren't on duty.'

Dimly, recollection returned. 'Oh—yes, of course. Sorry, I'm not thinking very clearly at the moment.'

'No, you're not. Bed, now,' Finn said firmly. 'I'll pick you up just before twelve, all right?'

Nodding, beyond argument or rational thought, she let them out, closed the door and slumped down on to the mat. She would go to bed in a minute. Just now, she was too relieved to be alone to bother to move. . .

CHAPTER SIX

By the time Finn had collected the Discovery, driven home and changed into warm dry clothes it was ten o'clock. He thought it would be a good idea to check Janna before he went to bed, because her temperature had dropped to less than thirty-six and really she should have been in hospital. Short of admitting her at that stage, he had done the only thing he could to warm her slowly and thoroughly—rather too thoroughly at the end.

He felt the heavy surge of need sweep over him again, just thinking about her, and swore softly. How he had stopped himself he didn't know, but even in such provocative circumstances he couldn't have taken advantage of her vulnerability. She would have hated him for it, and one thing he didn't need was Janna hating him.

Not that she seemed too happy as it was.

He sighed. He never did seem to be able to get it right with her these days. There had been a time when they were on exactly the same wavelength, but some time, somehow, he must have done something that had damaged their relationship.

He wished he could remember, but the first inkling he had was of the Christmas just before his father died, after the summer of Janna's eighteenth birthday. She had been distinctly chilly towards him, at a time when Finn had suddenly found himself obsessed by her— not just seeking her company, but seeking her love, wanting to hold her, touch her, make love to her.

That was just after he'd started having the dream.

He turned into her drive, jerking his thoughts to a halt. He couldn't think about the dream now, about the shadowed image of Janna lying in his arms under the stars in the barn at Camas Ciuicharan, her body warm and supple, naked in the moonlight, and her cries—just like the cries she had made earlier. . .

Damn. He shifted uncomfortably in his jeans, the images too powerful to ignore. He knew her so well that the Janna of his dreams was the real woman, not just a figment of his imagination. That made it all the harder to dismiss.

He could have made love to her earlier this evening. She had been there, his for the asking, begging with him. Anyone else would have ignored the voice of reason and taken what she had offered so sweetly. Not him—oh, no. Too damn busy being noble. He dropped his head on to the steering-wheel and groaned.

He wanted her. Every time he was with her, every time he touched her, smelt the faint scent of her perfume, heard her soft laughter, need stalked his body and left him hard and aching.

But he wasn't prepared to make love to her while she was still blowing hot and cold—one minute distant, the next all over him, as though she didn't want to want him but couldn't help herself.

No. Before he made love to her he wanted her to love him, as he loved her.

He had loved her for years, probably since he had walked into the kitchen of her parents' house, when she was four weeks old and screaming, and had picked her up and taken her out into the garden in the shade of the apple tree and sung to her, cradled on his grubby knees and staring at him with fixed green-grey eyes, mesmerised by his made-up lullaby.

He still remembered the tanning the cook gave him. She came barrelling out into the garden, flapping her voluminous white apron and shrieking, 'You durty wee urchin, what are you doing wi' ma bairn? How dare you lay a finger on her? Look at you, you grubby wee rascal!' She snatched the startled baby away from him and bore her, screaming, back into the kitchen. Moments later she came back out, picked Finn up by the scruff of the neck, bent him over her knee and larruped him until he could hardly stand.

It was too late, though, because while Finn had sat and stared into those fascinated little eyes, he had lost his heart.

As she grew, so he would watch her, from a distance. He became her keeper whenever he was around, and a good job he did. When she was even as young as two he rescued her from a pond. When she was four he climbed a tree and lifted her down. At five he helped her off the roof of the stable-block, at eight he followed her up the hill behind the house and convinced her not to run away. She had been reading *Huckleberry Finn*, and for a while she called him that. She thought it was very funny, and her delicious little giggle followed her taunting words.

Finn never minded, though. He always had time for the mischievous little scamp, and as she grew so they became constant companions. Both only children, they were inseparable, and Finn felt he knew her as well as he knew himself; as they matured and their understanding of each other grew, so their feelings deepened.

There might also have been an element of forbidden

fruit in their relationship, as well. He wasn't certain her parents had approved wholeheartedly of their friendship. Her father hadn't seemed to mind, but he'd had the feeling her mother looked down on him. His own family circumstances were far more modest, although he had never felt ashamed of his simple home.

He gave a wry chuckle now, thinking of Mrs Murray preferring to eat in the kitchen. His own family had no choice in their little croft. He had thought nothing of sitting in the kitchen with Janna as a child, drinking milk and eating Mrs Smith's home-made cookies, but he'd never gone beyond the door.

Finn remembered the first time he'd been past the kitchen in Janna's house, and chuckled.

She'd been fifteen, and there had been a huge trout in a glass case in the attic she'd said she wanted to show him. It had been just after he'd taught her to tickle trout, and he'd made the mistake of kissing her on the riverbank. Then, like a fool, he'd gone with her up the back stairs, and when they were in the attic she'd kissed him again.

There, in the steaming hot space under the rafters, amid the old trunks and broken furniture and a rocking-horse that had lost one ear, she looped her arms round his neck, drew his head down and kissed him full on the mouth.

He was so startled that he did nothing for a second, but then her sweet lips overwhelmed him and he kissed her back. He nearly lost his head, but then he heard a creak on the stairs and leapt away from her, just as Mrs Smith, the intimidating cook, panted into the doorway.

'Wha' are you doing up here wi' Janna, young McGregor?' she asked in her sergeant-major voice.

Finn was speechless, reduced again to a five-year-old, caught holding a tiny baby in the garden. Janna came to his rescue.

'We're looking for that old trout,' she said calmly. 'Oh, here it is. Look, Finn, isn't it amazing?'

He could hardly see straight, but he dutifully admired it. Then Janna pounced on something else.

'Oh, look, an old picnic basket. Smithie, do you think you would be able to clean it up? I'd love to have a picnic!'

Mrs Smith eyed them both suspiciously, took the picnic basket from Janna and hustled them both down the stairs.

'Imagine,' Janna whispered wickedly. 'Two old trout in the attic!'

Finn considered himself lucky to get away without another tanning.

After that he took care not to put himself in a situation with her where she could catch him unawares. He still kissed her occasionally, but only on his terms, when he felt relatively sure that things wouldn't get out of control—and never, absolutely never, at Glenmorriston House.

Her sudden change of attitude that Christmas she was eighteen was a real shock to Finn. He was invited up to the party on Christmas Eve, and Janna looked so beautiful he wanted to drag her away there and then. Instead he teased her, and chucked her under the chin, and she looked him straight in the eye for a second, then turned and walked away. She danced the rest of the evening with a lad from Craigmore. Finn was certain he'd seen him hanging around with her friends earlier in the year. Finn had wondered then if anything serious had developed between them. He didn't think so, but clearly she wasn't interested in *him* at the moment.

He cut his losses and went back to Edinburgh, nursing his wounds and kicking himself for leaving it too late. He would have to bide his time and try again when she had grown bored with the gangly, pimply youth from Craigmore.

When rumour told him that the boy had moved away, he decided to go back and see her and lay his feelings on the line.

However, he hadn't done so, because the next time he came home was because his father had been lost at sea, and Janna was away. She came back for the memorial service but didn't stay afterwards, and when he needed her she had gone again, back to Inverness.

Since then he hadn't seen her more than a few times, and every time she had been distant.

Now, though, he thought, the time had come to talk, to sort things out and find out how they really felt— or at least how Janna felt about him.

He knew how he felt about her. That had never been in doubt.

He got out of the car and headed for the door, knocked and listened. There were no lights on and the house was in silence, so she had probably gone to bed. Still, he ought to check she had locked up properly. He turned the handle and the door opened slightly, then he felt a resistance. He pushed gently, and a little moan came from the other side of the door. A chill whispered through him.

'Janna?'

There was another moan, and, not wasting a second, Finn ran round to the back door. It too was unlocked. After letting himself in, he ran through to the hall and found Janna, slumped against the front door.

Fear and guilt swamped him. Why had he left her? He should have taken better care of her at the beach, made sure she didn't get chilled, and then later. He should have sent her to the hospital, if not in the helicopter then as soon as he'd realised she was so cold. And now—damn it—now she was unconscious, and it was his fault, and if anything happened to her he would never forgive himself. He knelt beside her, taking her pulse, talking to her, checking her eyes for reflexes until she blinked sleepily.

'What are you doing here?' she mumbled.

Relief rippled through him, stealing his breath. 'Are you all right?' he asked, trying to keep his voice calm.

She sat up, slowly and a little stiffly. 'Of course. Why shouldn't I be?'

He let out his breath on a sigh 'You're on the floor in the hall. I left you nearly an hour ago; you've been here ever since.'

'I was tired,' she said, and her voice sounded thin and exhausted.

Finn didn't hesitate. Sliding his arms under her, he scooped her up, carried her up the stairs and undressed her, scolding her gently all the while, then tugged a nightie over her head and slid her under the covers, already asleep again. She would be all right, he realised with relief, but she needed supervision.

He went downstairs, rang his mother and told her where he was, then settled down on the sofa again, still fully dressed. It was quite comfortable—a bit full of memories, but at least it was downstairs and she was up, and maybe this way he would be able to keep his hands off her.

* * *

In the early hours of the morning she came to him in his dreams, her eyes laughing, her touch gentle, her hands magical, driving him wild. He woke shaking, his breath coming in short gasps, his body frustrated and tormented by the images.

He rolled on to his back and stabbed his hands through his hair in despair. He couldn't go on like this. The need for her was driving him crazy. He hadn't slept through the night once in the two weeks since he'd come back, and it was getting worse.

Sighing heavily, he threw the rug aside and went into the kitchen to make himself a drink. Their mugs from earlier on were still sitting there dirty, so while the kettle boiled he washed and dried them. He had just put the last one away when he heard a creak on the stairs.

Damn. He must have disturbed Janna. He opened the door and had a fleeting glimpse of something moving very fast, then there was a thump and a little cry of dismay, and pain splintered inside his head.

'Dammit, Janna, what the hell was that for?' he growled, clutching his tender skull in both hands and feeling cautiously for the egg that was no doubt forming.

He opened one eye and regarded her balefully. She was leaning against the door, a hefty book in her hands, and her eyes were like saucers.

'Are you all right?' she asked warily.

'I'll live.'

She put the book down on the kitchen table and came over to him, taking his head in her hands and bending him over so she could feel for the egg.

'Ouch,' he muttered.

'Sorry. You need ice on that.' She bustled about,

getting a gel-pack out of the fridge. After pushing him
down into a chair at the kitchen table she laid the pack
over the rapidly swelling bump and told him to hold
it in place.

'It's cold,' he grumbled.

'Mmm. It's meant to be. I'm awfully sorry, I thought
you were a burglar, creeping around like that in the
middle of the night.'

'And you were going to take me on with a
copy of——' he hefted the book '——*The Manual of
Paediatric Nursing?*'

'It's heavy,' she said lamely.

'I noticed.'

She bit her lip, and Finn noticed that as well as
remorse, laughter was dancing in those lovely
grey-green eyes.

He couldn't be cross with her, not when she was so
lovely, all rumpled and flushed with sleep, with a
crease in one cheek and her eyes sparkling with
mischief.

'You can atone for your sins by making me a cup
of tea and some toast,' he told her, and tried to drag
his eyes away from the smooth curve of her bottom
as she bent forward to reach the cups. They wouldn't
co-operate. 'Oh, what the hell,' he muttered under his
breath, and watched her anyway as she put the bread
in the toaster.

'Did you say something?' she asked.

'No. Janna, we need to talk about what happened
earlier.'

Was it his imagination, or did her shoulders
stiffen?

'Later. I want to have another look at your head,'
she told him. She took the gel-pack off and parted his

hair, examining the bump while Finn tried and failed to ignore the soft swell of her breasts just inches from his face. His body reacted predictably, and he closed his eyes with a groan.

'It's coming up nicely,' she told him, and he nearly choked on his laughter.

'What's funny?'

'Nothing,' he told her wryly. 'Nothing at all.'

She smoothed his hair back from his face, then hesitated, frowning. 'You've got a scar.'

'Mmm.'

Her finger traced the faint line on his temple. 'I don't remember it. Was that another foiled attempt at breaking and entering?'

He chuckled. 'Hardly. I smacked my head on the steering-wheel—about seven years ago, I suppose. I got it just after your birthday. I had a minor disagreement with a drunk driver on the Stirling road.'

She sat down and looked at him. 'You never told me that.'

He shrugged. 'It was nothing serious,' he said, playing down the accident that had put him in hospital for nearly a week. 'I'd just started my new job, and I was busy. I just got on with it—actually, it was a good excuse to replace my old banger with something that would start in the mornings! Anyway, it's hardly my first scar—I got worse cuts than that going through Mrs Cameron's hedge.'

Janna giggled, and Finn felt his heart ache. If only she was like this all the time. . .

They ate mounds of hot buttered toast and drank their tea in a companionable silence, Finn watching Janna over the top of his cup, and when they were finished he covered her hand with his.

'Janna, are you all right now?' he asked.

She nodded, but she didn't meet his eyes. 'Yes, I'm fine. The sleep's done me good.'

His thumb idly brushed the back of her hand. 'I'm sorry I let you get so cold. I should have thought about it earlier.'

She stared at him in amazement. 'Finn, you aren't my keeper! *I* should have thought of it. I'm a nurse, I've got enough knowledge about hypothermia and exposure without needing a nanny. I was stupid.'

'You were busy saving a life.'

'So were you. Finn, I'm fine, really.'

'You were cold,' he said gruffly. 'Your temperature was thirty-five point four. Really you should have gone to Fort William.'

She smiled, and his insides curled. 'So you said. Finn, I'm OK.' She blushed and looked away. 'Thank you for looking after me.'

'It was the least I could do.' He squeezed her hand. 'Why don't you get back to bed, and I'll go home now I know you're all right. OK? I'll collect you tomorrow in time for lunch.'

'There's no need,' she argued, but he didn't want her driving. Anyway, it was an excuse to be with her, and the way she was behaving just now he needed excuses.

'Don't argue,' he told her placidly. 'I'll be here.'

'Fuss-pot.'

'Undoubtedly. Goodnight, sweetheart.'

Unable to resist it, he pulled her gently into his arms and kissed her, dragging himself away when it threatened to overheat. Then he let himself out, drove home, fell into bed and dreamed of her again.

*   *   *

In the end Finn's plan to collect her came to nothing, because she had to visit old Mac McDougall after one of the carers phoned her at eight to say she'd found him on the floor.

Strictly speaking, she wasn't on duty, but he was one of her regular patients and she didn't really mind. She rang Finn, spoke to his mother and told her where she was going, and then left before he had time to ring her back.

She arrived at Mac's house to find him back in bed, but very chilled after lying on the floor for some unspecified time. His catheter was out again, and this time his urethra was split and bleeding and there was no way she could put another in.

'Mac, my love, you're going to have to go into the nursing home in Craigmore until you're a little better,' she told him gently.

'Och, noooo—dinnae send me there, lassie. Please, Sister, no that,' he begged, tears filling his rheumy old eyes.

Janna sighed. 'I'll get Dr McGregor to have a look at you, but I really think this time——'

Just then the doorbell rang, and she went to answer it, to find Finn standing there, bag in hand. 'Problems?' he asked.

'Fallen out of bed and torn his catheter out again.'

Finn sighed. 'Janna, he's got to go into a home. This can't go on much longer.'

'So you tell him. He won't listen to me.'

Finn squeezed past her in the little hallway and went into the bedroom, perching on the edge of the bed and taking Mac's withered old hand. 'Hello, there,' he said with a smile. 'I'm Dr McGregor.'

Mac frowned. 'Dr MacWhirter no on today?'

'No, he's retired now. I've taken over from him.'

The old man peered at him. 'I remember you—you're Dougal's boy, aren't you?' he said, in a moment of lucidity.

Finn nodded. 'Yes, that's right.'

'Terrible waste, that. Awful shame.'

'Aye, it was,' Finn agreed quietly.

'He'd be proud of you, son,' Mac told him in a thready voice.

'Not if I can't persuade you to let me look after you, he wouldn't,' Finn replied with a wry grin. 'Now, Mac, what are we going to do wi' you?'

'Leave me to die in peace,' he pleaded. 'A body has a right to die where he wants.'

'But, Mac, you aren't dying. You just need to be cared for better than we can manage for you at home. It was all right for a while, but now you need more care. You don't want to lie on the floor for hours, freezing to death in the winter, do you? And wouldn't you be happier with a bit of company?'

'What would I want wi' company? Lot of daft auld hens clucking away all the time—nae, laddie. I'll be right fine here, in ma own home.'

'Why are they all so damn stubborn in this part of the world?' Finn asked later, after they had cleaned him up, stuck a urine bag on and left him, with the next carer due an hour later.

They had gone in convoy to Janna's parents', and were now seated in the kitchen at Glenmorriston House sipping sherry, while Janna's mother checked the joint and Janna laid the huge old refectory table.

Janna's father laughed. 'Are the locals giving you trouble, Finn?'

He rolled his eyes. 'I'll say. Mrs Buchan won't go

into a home, even though she's totally doo-lally, Mac's bedridden, incontinent and as stubborn as an old goat, and Lindsay Baird nearly killed herself and the babe not going to hospital for the birth. Yet in Edinburgh they're trying every trick in the book to get themselves admitted!'

'They don't want to be away from their relatives,' Mrs Murray said. 'It's quite reasonable. They're so used here to coping with their own problems and falling back on their own resources, they don't like it when they lose their independence.'

'I'd noticed,' Finn said drily.

'You can't blame them, Finlay,' Jessie McGregor said. 'Would you want to go into a home?'

'No—but I wouldn't want to lie on the floor for hours in a pool of urine and wonder when I was going to be rescued, either. Nor does that excuse explain Lindsay Baird. No, there's something in the water,' he said with a twinkle.

Janna laughed. 'Well, let me tell you it doesn't seem to affect the visitors. We've had more carted off to hospital this year than I can remember. I'm just waiting for a nice asthma attack now they've started haymaking over towards Inverbeg. That'll be the next thing.'

'How jolly. Janna, darling, would you make the gravy? Finn, help yourself to sherry and keep your mother topped up. George, could you find a nice bottle of red to go with the venison, please?'

'All done,' Janna's father said, stretching out his legs and draining his sherry-glass. 'So, Jessie, is it good to have Finn home again?'

Jessie's eyes softened. 'Och, yes—you can have no idea how I missed him, especially since Dougal——' She broke off, lifting her shoulders in a sad little shrug, and Finn reached across and squeezed her hand.

'Well, you're stuck wi' me now, Mother. I'm home for guid,' he said, his brogue more pronounced with the emotion he was trying to disguise.

Jessie covered his hand with her other one and patted it. 'And very welcome, too. Now all I need is some grandchildren to fuss over.'

Janna froze, her hand on the gravy spoon, her heart stopped, waiting for Finn's reply while pain ripped through her. Jessie should have had grandchildren by now—one, at least. . .

'One thing at a time, Mother,' he said lightly. 'I think perhaps I should get married first, don't you?'

Janna felt everyone's eyes swivel to her back. Mechanically, unable to think or speak, she stirred the gravy like a robot, until her mother removed the pan with a click of her tongue and poured the dehydrated remains into the gravy boat.

'Janna, what are you thinking about?' she scolded gently. 'The gravy's nearly all boiled away! I'll have to top it up.'

'I'm sorry,' she murmured. 'I was miles away.'

Miles away in Inverness, at the beginning of October, ten weeks after her eighteenth birthday, waking up to the enormity of her loss. Finn hadn't contacted her, all his words had been empty promises, and now the last link with him was gone in a haze of pain and despair. Swamped by the memory, she headed blindly for the door.

'I think I need a little air,' she said. Excusing herself, she went out into the garden, to the shade under the apple tree, sinking down on to the ground with her arms wrapped round her waist, holding in the pain. Gradually, in the cool, quiet shade, she felt it recede to the dull ache that was with her all the time.

Behind her she felt Finn approach, his quiet tread inaudible on the grass.

There was so much he didn't know, so much she really ought to tell him. If he had made love to her yesterday, she would have told him. But he hadn't. Instead he had walked away from her again, rejecting her again, hurting her again.

Damn. Why did she still love him, want him?

'Are you all right?'

She nodded. 'A bit hot, that's all. I expect my temperature regulation will be a bit up the spout for a day or two after yesterday. Is lunch ready?'

'Yes. Your mother sent me to fetch you in.'

Janna sighed. Her mother, once opposed to Finn, was now enchanted by the man he had become, and able to forgive him his humble origins because of his cleverness and qualifications.

Her father had always liked and respected Finn, and his father before him. Her mother had merely tolerated them—until now. Now, Janna guessed, she was making a big effort to cultivate the man she imagined was about to become her son-in-law.

If only Janna could be so certain. As it was, she thought it seemed highly unlikely. If he still wanted to marry her, he would hardly have turned down an invitation as blatant as last night's!

She realised Finn was holding down his hand to her, and, taking it, she pulled herself up, plastered what could have been a smile on her face and turned and went back into the kitchen.

The problem of what to do with Mac was solved that night, because he suffered a massive stroke and died shortly before the ambulance reached him, in his home, as he had wanted.

Finn was saddened, but relieved for him that he hadn't been forced to suffer a protracted failing. He had been ninety-three, after all, and until very recently apparently had been able to care for himself. It was what he would have wanted.

Finn broke the news to Janna the next morning, when he arrived at her house for surgery, having been contacted by Heather Glennie, the relief doctor who covered his weekends and night-calls on rota. He had gone to see Mac, because he was much nearer than Heather, and had been with him at the end.

'It was very peaceful—he just slowed down and stopped breathing, and quietly slipped away.'

'Oh,' Janna said. 'I suppose it's a relief.' And she went back into her room. Finn followed her, turned her into his arms and let her cry.

'You're an old softie,' he murmured into her hair.

'He was sweet.'

'Aye. Well, at least he wasn't miserable.'

'Mmm. I'll cross him off my list,' she said, and pushed gently out of his arms.

Finn let her go, went back into the consulting-room and saw his patients, then headed back to the main surgery and dispensary in Craigmore to update files before his afternoon surgery.

While he was there he pulled out Janna's file, to make a note of her mild hypothermia. Now, how was he going to describe her treatment? he thought with a chuckle.

He pulled the notes out of the envelope, and the smile died on his lips.

Spontaneous abortion—twelve weeks' dur-
ation—October.

He counted, then checked again. Seven years ago—
she must have conceived during the summer of her
eighteenth birthday, he thought numbly. He sat down,
his legs like jelly. So it was true. She had had an affair
with the lad from Craigmore. What was his name?
Michael? Matthew? It didn't matter, they'd moved
away long ago.

Finn stared at the notes, scanned the letter from the
hospital and sat back in his chair, totally numbed. His
Janna, his sweet, precious, mischievous Janna had got
into trouble while he wasn't there to look after her.
She never had known when she was playing with fire.
Look how she had flirted with him when she was fifteen
or so. Anyone less careful for her would have found
the invitation irresistible—anyone like that stringy lad
from Craigmore.

'Bastard,' he muttered. And then the pain hit him,
the terrible, biting jealousy. If it had had to be someone, then why not him? Why Michael/Matthew, a
seven-day wonder, with muscles like knots in cotton
and a mind to match?

Anger ripped through him. Damn her. How could
she have done that—to him and to herself?

Thank God the baby had been lost before it could
ruin her life. Stuffing the notes back into the envelope,
he put them back into the file drawer and turned his
attention to the repeat prescriptions for the Kilbarchan
residents. They would go out with the delivery that
afternoon. He had to print them so the dispenser could
get them ready.

He gazed blankly at the computer screen. Damn

her. How could she? He would have to stay away from her for a few days, until he could think rationally about it. Otherwise he might just kill her.

Jessie's ulcer was improving, and Janna was delighted. She had been so worried about it, but now the debriding paste had cleaned the area back to fresh, raw skin and the tissue was starting to granulate nicely. Maybe now it would begin to heal properly, at last.

'I did enjoy lunch wi' your parents, Janna,' Jessie said as Janna worked. 'Such lovely people. My Dougal always spoke very highly of your father.'

Janna smiled. 'It was mutual. He lost a friend in your husband, Jessie—a good friend.'

Jessie nodded. 'Aye—we all did. I wish they'd found him so we had something to lay to rest. I think that's the worst. Not knowing.'

Janna laid the clean collagen dressing over the ulcer and pressed it firmly on. 'He couldn't be in a more beautiful place, Jessie,' she said gently.

Jessie sighed. 'Aye, I know.' She pulled herself up visibly, and smiled at Janna. 'The barn will be wonderful, won't it?'

Janna nodded. 'Finn showed it to me on Saturday. It will be lovely.'

'A bit remote for his job, but I suppose it doesn't take so very long to get there from here.'

'Only twenty minutes—less if you're in a real hurry, or at night when you can see the lights coming.' In fact, Janna had thought the barn was a bit far out. Most doctors tried to live centrally to their practice. At the barn Finn would be about ten miles west of the centre of his, and ten miles on those roads was quite significant, especially in an emergency.

Still, miles in that remote part of the Scottish Highlands tended to be something taken for granted anyway. Janna certainly did far more miles than her city colleagues.

In fact, now Finn had bought the barn, Janna supposed she could use her grandmother's money to buy a newer car. Finn's Discovery was perfect for the job— a bit heavy on fuel compared to Betsy, but much more comfortable, and far more sensible in the winter. Although with the sea on two sides, as it was on the peninsula, and with the benefit of the Gulf Stream, hard winters were less likely than in the hills inland.

She would have to think about it.

It occurred to her that she still hadn't paid Finn for the damage to his lights when he had swerved off the road to avoid her that first day he was back. She must mention it to him again. She had noticed some new crash bars on the front of the car—was that in self-defence, in case she did the same thing again?

Probably. Well, he should have taught her to drive better. Obviously it was his fault.

She packed up her things, made them both a cup of tea and sat sipping it while Jessie talked about Finn, and old Mac McDougall, and what they could do about Betty Buchan.

'Couldn't you get her to help with the Seniors' Lunch Club? Could she lay the tables or something? She's such a busy person, if she had a purpose maybe she'd be more settled.'

'I'll ask the others,' Jessie said. 'Oh, there's Finn come home. Is there another cup in the pot, Janna?'

'I'm sure there is.' She stood up and went to the kitchen and poured a cup of tea, turning with it in her hand as he strode down the hall.

'Tea for you,' she said, and then faltered at the look in his eyes. She had never seen them so cold and remote.

'I thought you would have finished by now. It's late,' he growled.

Janna's hand shook, and the tea slopped into the saucer. She set it down with exaggerated care. What was wrong? Whatever it was, she thought, he didn't want her here, that much was sure.

'I'm just going,' she told him. 'I'll leave your tea here.' She squeezed past him—not that it was hard, the way he flattened himself against the wall—and picked up her bag.

'Going so quickly?' Jessie said, surprised. 'Stay and have a cup of tea with Finn, love.'

'No, really, I have to go,' Janna said quickly, and, grabbing her things, she kissed Jessie's cheek and escaped down the hall.

Finn followed her, his mood almost palpable. 'There's no need for you to come here, I'm quite capable of doing an ulcer dressing,' he told her. 'I'll pick up some stuff from the surgery and do it myself in future.'

'But it's no trouble——'

'I said, I'll do it.'

Janna was chilled by his tone.

'Fine,' she replied stiffly. 'Goodnight.'

There was no reply.

She got into her car, reversed out into the lane and drove home, puzzled and confused by Finn's sudden coldness. What had happened? Only this morning he had been holding her in his arms while she cried, and now this evening he had acted as though she had some vile disease!

She ran a hot bath, climbed into it and lay down, still thinking about Finn and his abrupt about-face. Ridiculous to feel so hurt. He was probably preoccupied by a patient.

But she knew he wasn't. Finn had never—never—looked at her like that.

A hiccuping sob rose in her throat, and she stood up and scrubbed herself roughly all over. Damn him, she wouldn't cry. She wouldn't. . .

Sinking back into the water, she bit her lip and let the tears fall.

CHAPTER SEVEN

THE next time she saw Finn he was less terrifyingly cold, but still distant. Janna could only assume that he was cross with himself for having allowed their intimacy on Saturday night, and had pulled back from what he must have realised was a mistake—just as he had before.

The only difference was that before he had simply taken himself off. Now he was there, working with her, and clearly regretting it.

She could have allowed herself to go to pieces. It would have been very easy, but she was made of sterner stuff. She had got through his rejection once before, and forewarned was forearmed.

She had been expecting this all along, ever since he had kissed her at MacWhirter's farewell party. It was hardly a surprise. What was a surprise was that it could still hurt so much. But, Janna being Janna, she shrugged it off and carried on by doing her usual.

She avoided him whenever possible.

It worked for a couple of days, but then they were thrown together in an emergency, and had no choice but to communicate.

Mrs Buchan, their confused elderly resident, stood on a chair to change a lightbulb and fell off, shattering a mirror and cutting herself badly. She rang Moira at the shop, and Janna was fortunately at home and went straight there, leaving Moira tracking Finn down at

Glenmorriston, where he should just have finished his morning surgery.

By the time Janna arrived Mrs Buchan was extremely weak, and Janna instantly saw why. A shard of mirror had slashed the right side of her neck and blood was welling freely from the site—welling and also, if she wasn't mistaken, pulsing slightly. Janna propped her up so that her neck was supported on a pillow, with a ring pad around the wound to reduce the bleeding, rolled up her sleeve and inserted a giving set into the vein on the back of her left forearm, taping it down in readiness for the plasma expander that Finn carried with him at all times.

There was a nasty cut on the back of her right upper arm which was also bleeding quite freely still, and Janna was about to dress it when she heard a car skid to a halt on the loose stones by the road, then the door slammed and Finn was in beside her. Betty was weakening fast and, without wasting time on conversation, Finn set up a drip, opened the valve and let it run in flat-out.

'Where can we hang this?' he asked, looking round.

Janna found an old standard lamp, unplugged it and removed the shade and hung the drip pack from the bulb-holder. 'OK?'

'Fine. Right, we need to get her to hospital fast. Have you called Inverness?'

She shook her head. 'I didn't have time. I thought the drip should go in first.'

He nodded, then picked up Mrs Buchan's phone and called the Raigmore in Inverness.

'They're out on a call,' he said, frustration edging his voice. 'They can't get here for two hours, and she can't wait that long. I'll call Hughie.'

'Hughie?' Janna asked, puzzled.

'Aye—lives on Eigg. He's got a helicopter—he owes me a favour. He can take us.'

He dialled again, spoke briefly, then set the receiver down. 'He's on his way. We have to make an H on the nearest piece of flat ground—how about the field behind the house?'

Janna nodded. 'I'll go and find some sheets and lay it out—you stay here and look after Betty. There's a nasty cut on the underneath of her right arm that could do with a dressing and a pressure pad, too.'

'OK, I'll see to it. Weight the sheets down—you don't want them tangling in the rotors.'

'How long have I got?' she asked.

'Ten minutes, at most.'

'Right.'

Leaving Betty Buchan in his care while he dealt with her arm, Janna grabbed all the linen she could find in the airing-cupboard, went out of the back door and scanned the field. There were rocks in most of it, but there was one area that just might be flat enough to land.

'I hope he's a good pilot,' she muttered, and, spreading out the sheets, she made the biggest H she could manage, with the bar centred on the flattest piece of ground. Just as she was finishing she heard the rhythmic slap of the rotors in the air, and went back in to Finn.

'He's coming. How is she?'

'Going down fast. We'll have to elevate her legs and arms to pool the blood in her trunk or her circulation'll collapse. She's perilously close as it is. I think she might have grazed the wall of her carotid artery—if it goes, she will too. Go and see Hughie down.'

Janna ran out again, waving to the helicopter that was circling in view now, and then waited with bated breath until it touched down safely.

As the rotors slowed, Hughie jumped out and ran towards her. 'Hi! Where's the patient?'

'Inside,' she said economically, and turned and ran for the door.

Finn was just changing the bag of plasma expander as they went in, squeezing the bag in by hand.

'God, what a blood-bath!' Hughie exclaimed. 'You are coming with me, aren't you?'

Finn shot him a grin. 'I think it might be a good idea, don't you? Here, grab her feet, and Janna, bring the drip. We need to move fast.' Between them, Finn and Hughie lifted the slender, unconscious form of Mrs Buchan and carried her to the waiting helicopter while Janna steadied her head and held the bag of plasma up. Once in the tiny cockpit, Janna fixed a makeshift hook for the bag while Finn and Hughie supported Mrs Buchan on cushions, so that her legs were elevated and her head propped firmly. Delay now could be fatal, Janna knew, and she wondered how fast Hughie could fly.

'Right, Janna, could you call ahead to the hospital, get them ready with some universal donor and tell them she'll need at least four units stat, followed by whatever, once they can cross-match. Tell them the glass has penetrated the jugular vein and might have nicked the carotid artery, the patient's unconscious and failing fast. Hughie, how long will we be?'

'About half an hour, perhaps a little more,' he said.

Janna nodded, jumped down out of the helicopter and turned back to Finn. 'I'll get your car back to my house—Hughie can land in the school playing-field when he brings you back.'

Finn nodded, slammed the door to, and Janna retreated out of range of the rotors.

The little craft rose smoothly, turned east and headed away, the beat of the rotors fading gradually.

Janna watched until it was little more than a dot in the sky, and then went back in to deal with the chaos.

It took her some time to sweep up the broken glass and clear up the blood. There was a mark she thought would never come out of the carpet, but she couldn't spend too long because she had other patients to deal with and she had already lost over an hour. Let Mrs Buchan's relatives deal with it, she thought crossly. They did little enough to help the poor old woman.

She had to go to see Lindsay Baird, whom she was still visiting every day, and for once she was unable to find time for the cup of tea and cuddle with the babe that she usually managed to fit in.

Not that it was all a pleasure. Holding the baby brought the bitter-sweet pain of loss, and Lindsay's sole topic of conversation seemed to be Finn and how Janna was getting on with him. As she really wasn't, it was quite useful to have an excuse to escape that day and go back to her house to catch up with paper-work after her calls were done.

She thought Finn and Hughie would be hungry, so she bought a flan from the shop and threw a salad together. She had just finished when the doorbell rang, and she opened the door to find young Sophie standing there, almost completely concealed by a bunch of flowers, and her father with a bottle of whisky in his hand.

'Thank you for helping me,' Sophie said shyly, and

pushed the flowers towards Janna.

'Oh, sweetheart—how lovely! Well, thank you very much,' she said, bending and kissing the soft little cheek. 'So, how are you, darling? How's your poor wee foot?'

Sophie held it out so that Janna could see the scrapes, now healing nicely. 'It wasn't broked. I just cut it.'

'Oh, I am glad,' Janna said, throwing a smile up at the little girl's father. 'I hope it hasn't completely ruined your holiday?'

'Not as completely as if you hadn't been there,' he said drily. 'Really, we can't thank you enough. I wonder if you could pass this on to Dr McGregor with our thanks?' He gave her the bottle, and Janna took it with a smile.

'Thank you all very much. It really wasn't necessary——'

'Rubbish. It's just a token. Come on, Sophie, let's go and find the others now.'

'Bye,' Janna called after them. 'Enjoy the rest of your holiday.'

'We will,' Sophie called, waving over her shoulder.

Janna watched them out of sight, then put the flowers in the sink and stood the bottle on the worktop to give Finn. She had just finished arranging the flowers when she heard the helicopter returning. It was early evening, the sun still high in the sky, and she thought Hughie was bound to come in for a rest. However, moments later, she heard the helicopter as it took off, and when she went to the door she saw Finn trudging up the road towards her house. He looked tired, but, more than that, he looked defeated.

Janna ran down the drive to meet him. 'How is she?' she asked, sure from his appearance that they must have lost her.

'Oh, she'll do. Very weak, but they've transfused her and she's much stronger now.'

'Oh, thank God—you looked so down, Finn.'

He met her eyes. 'Did I?' he said bleakly. 'I've been thinking about things. Can I come in?'

She nodded, wondering what he had been thinking about that had made him look so grim. 'Of course. I made supper—I thought Hughie might stay.'

'He had to get back to his farm, but I'm starving.'

'Good,' she said. Whatever was wrong? He looked so troubled. She led him into the kitchen, put the kettle on and then remembered the presents.

'Here,' she said, holding out the bottle of ten-year-old single malt whisky. 'This is for you, from Sophie's parents. They brought me the flowers, too.'

'How kind of them.' He took the bottle, examined the label and twisted off the cap, sniffing appreciatively. 'Is the sun over the yard-arm yet?'

Janna laughed. 'I should think so. It would be further south.' She reached him down a heavy tumbler.

'Join me,' he said, and after a second's hesitation she took down another glass from the cupboard.

'Just a very small one, then, to keep you company.'

He poured two measures, one small, the other considerably larger, recapped the bottle and pushed the smaller glass towards her. 'Cheers,' he said heavily, and, lifting the glass, he took a hefty swig, sighed, then peered at the glass thoughtfully. 'That is wonderful. How the hell did they know?' he murmured.

Janna sipped the malt and studied him. He looked so

preoccupied. After a second he seemed to pull himself together. 'So, how is Sophie?' he asked. 'Any fractures?'

Janna shook her head. 'No. Her foot's sore and swollen, but she doesn't seem to have suffered any ill-effects from the experience.' Unlike us, she nearly said, because since that day she seemed to have been riding an emotional rollercoaster with Finn.

She still didn't know what had happened on Monday to make him so angry with her. Because he had been angry; she knew that.

If only she had some idea.

She finished her whisky, noted that Finn's first glassful was drained and he was starting on the second, and thought it might be an idea to feed him if he was going to hit the bottle so vigorously.

She cleared the table and laid it, surreptitiously removing the bottle to the other side of the kitchen, and set the food down in front of a wryly smiling Finn.

'What's the matter, Janna? Afraid I'll finish the bottle?'

She was, but she didn't think it would be a good idea to say so. Instead she ignored him, fetching the flan from the larder and putting it on a mat, then cutting a huge chunk for Finn. 'Here, help yourself to salad.'

It seemed so strange, sitting down to eat with him and not knowing what had been going on in his mind that week. Clearly something significant had happened. No doubt he would say something when he was ready. Until then she would keep quiet and hope she could deal with it when the time came.

It came, quite out of the blue, later that evening.

They had adjourned to the sitting-room, Finn making himself at home without invitation, a third glass of whisky in his hand.

For a while he was silent, swirling the pale liquid round and round. Then he spoke, the words dropping into the silence like stones.

'Why didn't you tell me about the baby?'

Her breath jammed in her throat. 'Baby?' she said with commendable calm. 'What baby?' Dear God, he can't know! she thought. No one knows. I haven't told anyone, not even my mother!

'You had a miscarriage, seven years ago. It's in your notes.'

Of course. It was so obvious she nearly laughed out loud at her stupidity. 'Why were you looking in my notes?' she said, to give herself time.

'I thought I ought to enter the hypothermia.'

'Oh.'

'Yes, oh.' He put the glass down and steepled his fingers, lying back in the chair and watching her steadily over them. 'So, why didn't you tell me?'

Her body sagged in defeat. He knew now. She might as well tell him all of it.

'I tried to ring you, but you weren't there. Your flatmates said they'd get you to ring, but you didn't. I tried again a few days later, but again you were out.'

'You should have persevered.'

She laughed, a hollow, bitter little laugh. 'I did. I kept getting someone called Max, who told me he'd passed the message on and if I couldn't take the hint—— Well, in the end he was quite rude.' She twisted her hands together. 'I kept waiting for you to contact me, but you never did. Then I lost the baby, and after that there didn't seem any point in telling you. You didn't seem terribly interested in what was happening in my life or you would have returned my calls. I didn't want to be a nuisance.'

Finn sighed softly. 'Oh, Janna, you were never a nuisance.'

'That's not what your flatmate said. Anyway, I stopped ringing and just waited for you to contact me, but you never did.'

He sighed again, more heavily. 'I'm sorry. I was so busy—it was my first house job and I was rushed off my feet. I didn't get time to come home until Christmas, and I kept meaning to write but I just didn't get round to it. I was working a hundred and twenty hours a week sometimes, and my head was still giving me hell. When I wasn't on duty I was asleep.'

'You must have had some time off,' she said sceptically. 'You could have contacted me—damn it, it was August when I first rang. Couldn't you have found just five minutes to ring me before Christmas? I needed you, Finn,' she went on, her voice catching. 'Can you imagine what it's like to find out you're pregnant and then realise that the father doesn't give a damn——?' Her voice cracked, and she pressed her hand against her mouth, struggling not to break down. She wouldn't cry, she wouldn't!

Finn ran a hand through his hair, and the light gleamed dully on the faint line of the scar. 'Oh, hell, Janna—I'm sorry. What a mess, sweetheart.'

'The miscarriage was awful,' she whispered. 'I wanted that baby so much, you can have no idea. And then suddenly, one day, I woke up and it was gone—snuffed out before it even had a chance. I had to go in and have a D and C.'

Finn's brow creased in a frown of concern and he leant forward, taking her hands in his.

'Och, sweetheart, don't cry. There'll be other babies.'

She lifted her head and stared bleakly into his eyes. 'Will there? Aren't you forgetting something rather vital? Babies need a father, Finn—a father who loves them, who wants to be with them and doesn't get bored before he even knows of their existence!'

She snatched her hands away, curling up defensively in the far corner of the sofa, and Finn sat back with a sigh. 'I'm sorry I wasn't there for you when you needed me, Janna. Things really went awry after the accident. I might even have still been in hospital when you rang.'

She stared at him in confusion. 'You were admitted?' she said in surprise. 'I didn't realise that!'

He shrugged. 'It wasn't anything serious, just a few cuts and bruises and slight concussion—nothing to get excited about. It messed me up for quite a while, though. My short-term memory was wrecked for a bit—I had to be very careful when I was on duty to write everything down straight away, otherwise I overlooked things. I might even have had your message and not had time to ring straight away, and then forgotten. Perhaps that was why Max got so short with you.'

Janna stared at him, a sudden terrible suspicion forming in the back of her mind. A question hovered on the tip of her tongue, but she could hardly bring herself to ask it, because the answer could be devastating.

For a long time she was silent, then she dragged in

a steadying breath and looked up at him. 'Finn, when you said your short-term memory was wrecked—can you remember that summer, when you were here in July?'

He shook his head. 'No, not really. Patches, nothing more. I know I was here for your birthday, but I can't remember a minute of it. I had the accident a couple of weeks later and I've lost all of that time completely.'

Janna stared at him, her worst suspicions realised. If he didn't remember her birthday, then he probably didn't remember the weeks leading up to it—the laughter they'd shared, the fun they'd had—or after her party, when they had gone to Camas Ciuicharan and he had made love to her under the stars. All of it was gone, lost to him for all time. He didn't know they had made love, didn't know about the promises he had made and then broken—because, of course, they hadn't been broken.

He simply didn't know they existed. Which probably meant he didn't realise the baby she had lost was his.

She pressed her fingers to her brow, massaging away an ache that had started to form. He didn't know. He really didn't know.

But where did she go from here? How did she tell him about them? About their lovemaking? And, most particularly, about the baby?

He stood up. 'You're tired, Janna. I'll go now. I've got some notes to write up at home.'

She made to get up but he pushed her back gently. 'You stay there and rest. I'll let myself out. Thanks for supper.'

He kissed her cheek, patted it gently and then went,

leaving her sitting in the gathering gloom, her thoughts in chaos.

Where on earth did she go from here?

CHAPTER EIGHT

'So THERE you are—as far as I can tell, he doesn't remember anything of that summer.'

Lindsay Baird stared at Janna, her mouth slightly open with shock. 'None of it?' she asked finally.

Janna shrugged. 'Not as far as I know. It's hard to ask, isn't it? "Don't you remember when we all went on that picnic to the seal rock, and they all came and sang round us? How about the time we went for a walk and found the doe with her fawns, and we watched them for hours before they scented us and moved off? Do you remember that? All right, then, how about making love to me? Ring any bells?"'

Lindsay sighed. 'Yes, I can quite see how it's going to be tricky. Still, he's got to know.'

'But how?'

Her friend shrugged. 'Another cup of tea?'

'I'd love one—I'll make it, you should be resting. I don't really know what I'm doing here, dragging out all my problems when you've just a baby. I'm supposed to be looking after you, not wearing you out.'

'You aren't wearing me out, and you have been looking after me—not that I need it.' She grinned smugly. 'After such a straightforward delivery——'

'Your delivery was not straightforwad!' Janna protested. 'It was anything but! Has Fergus booked his vasectomy yet?'

Lindsay laughed. 'No—he's a coward. Anyway, I quite fancy four.'

Janna groaned. 'Just let me retire first, OK?'

'You might have your own by then.'

She went still, and something on her face must have alerted Lindsay, because she moved closer and laid her hand on Janna's shoulder.

'Is there something you aren't telling me? You didn't have an abortion, did you, after that summer?'

Janna shook her head. 'No. Not an abortion.'

'A miscarriage.' It wasn't a question, and Janna didn't answer. 'Oh, love, I'm sorry. You must have been devastated.'

'I needed him,' she said, her voice cracking. 'I really needed him, and he didn't even know. I was losing his child, and he didn't even know. . .' She took a steadying breath. 'That's going to be the hardest thing to tell him. I don't know how he'll react. I expect he'll say I should have written, but I wanted to tell him face to face. Instead, I didn't get the chance to tell him at all.'

Lindsay took over the tea-making, poured two mugs and towed Janna back out to the garden. The children were all in bed, even the baby was asleep. There was nothing to disturb them except the cry of the gulls over the sea and the distant drone of Fergus's tractor, working late into the evening, making hay.

'So,' Lindsay said, lowering herself into the sun-lounger and stretching her feet out, 'you need a plan.'

'Don't I just. But what?'

'How about staging a reconstruction? You know, like they do on *Crimewatch* and things like that? Take him to the same places, do the same things—try and jog his memory.'

'Do I tell him what I'm doing?'

Lindsay thought for a moment, then shook her head. 'No. No, I don't think so. It might make him try too hard. Just let the images flow over him.'

'And if it doesn't work?'

'It must. Look, Janna, it's the same time of year. When's your birthday? Next Friday? That's the day of the Kilbarchan Show. Finn's bound to go—he always has. Fergus has got sheep in the show, and he'll be doing the hill-run and tossing the sheaf and throwing the hammer. We'll get him in on this, get him to egg Finn on to do the same things. Can you remember what he did?'

Janna laughed wryly. 'Of course—I can remember every move he's ever made, I think.'

'Excellent. Right, that's settled. You'll hijack all his free time, organise him to death—you always used to, he won't think it's at all strange.'

Janna blushed. 'Was I really so pushy?'

'Pushy?' Lindsay giggled helplessly. 'Never, Janna! Whatever gave you that idea? No, you just organised us all out of existence. Come on. Do this. We're going there—never a moment's peace. Still, it was fun, because you always had wonderful ideas.'

Janna laughed awkwardly, not sure she liked the image Lindsay was painting. 'I'm sure they weren't. Anyway, my parents wouldn't agree with you. Most of the time I was growing up they had no idea where I was.'

'Probably just as well, I imagine,' Lindsay said drily. 'And if Finn hadn't always been such a gentleman, you probably would have been in much more trouble much younger! You were such a flirt.'

Janna's blush deepened. 'Oh, God, Lindsay, don't,' she moaned.

'He loved it—he loved *you*, Janna. He never looked at another girl. I'll never forget the look in his eyes at your birthday party. I'm surprised you both stayed as late as you did!'

'Lindsay, don't!' Janna buried her face in her hands. After a moment she lifted her head. 'How are we going to recreate that party? It'll be impossible.'

'Your parents could throw a little party for your birthday—us, and Finn, and his mother, and perhaps one or two of their friends—Bill and Helen MacWhirter, for instance. I'm sure we could create enough of an atmosphere if we tried. Of course, most of the others aren't here any more, but it might be enough by then. He will have had all the other reminders. Then all you have to do is drag him off at the end of the evening and seduce him. How's the barn coming on?'

Janna shrugged. 'I don't know. I haven't been down there this week. Why?'

'Because, dopey, you need to take him back there, and you need the roof open, like it was before. You'll have to get Angus to stop work—I'll get Fergus to bribe him. We need the roof of our house repaired before the winter comes, and there are one or two window frames that need attention—we'll steal him. Then he won't be able to do any more, and you can take Finn back there and recreate to your heart's content!'

Lindsay sat back, a smug matchmaker's smile on her face, and Janna sighed.

'You make it all sound so easy.'

'It is easy. Whether or not it works is another question.'

Just then they heard the sound of the tractor stop,

and a few minutes later Fergus pulled into the farmyard in his pick-up.

'Hello, ladies—any tea left for me?'

Lindsay wrinkled her nose delicately. 'Do you smell too bad?'

He laughed. 'Probably. I'll sit out of your way.'

'Well, not too far away. We've got something to tell you.'

He fetched himself a cup, sat as promised, on the other side of the patio, and looked at them expectantly. 'Well?'

They filled him in, leaving out the baby, and when they had finished he let out his breath in a low whistle. 'That's a hell of a task, bringing back someone's memory. What if he's blocked it out subconsciously because—sorry, Janna—because he can't cope with it? What if he made all those promises about marrying you in the heat of the moment, and just needed an escape route?'

'Fergus, you're going soft in the head!' Lindsay scoffed. 'He loves her!'

'Does he?'

Janna sighed. 'I don't know.'

'Why don't you take him out for a drink and get him talking?' Lindsay suggested to her husband. 'I'm sure you can find out.'

Fergus snorted. 'We're not like you women, you know. We don't all get together and discuss our sex-lives.'

Janna blushed furiously, and Lindsay threw a cobbled up tissue at him. 'We don't sit and talk about our sex-lives. We talk about the things that matter, the things that make life worth living——'

'I rest my case,' Fergus said with a smirk, and stood

up and went into the house. A few moments later he came out, showered and changed. 'Right, ladies, stage one going into operation. I'm meeting Finn now at the pub.'

'Don't you dare drink anything stronger than orange juice, Fergus Baird,' Lindsay threatened. 'Not if you're driving, and certainly not if it'll loosen your tongue! Finn's not to get a hint of what's going on.'

Fergus bent over and kissed his wife gently. 'Trust me, sweetheart. I do know what I'm doing. And don't wait up. If he starts talking, I'll let him run on.'

'Thank you, Fergus,' Janna said, jumping up and hugging him impulsively. 'Ring me when you get in—I don't care what time it is. I won't sleep till I know.'

He patted her awkwardly. 'Don't fret, lass. It'll come out right in the end. Just hang on.'

Janna, watching him go, hoped desperately that he was right.

Finn stared into the glass of beer, swirling it gently and studying the little eddies in the froth.

'Penny for them.'

Finn snorted. 'No way, friend. They're unprintable.'

Beside him Fergus stretched out, his long legs rivalling Finn's own, and regarded him with a speculative smile. 'Janna?' he offered quietly.

Finn avoided his eyes. The quiet farmer who had been his lifelong friend was too damn good at reading him.

'I always thought,' Fergus continued in the same soft, undemanding voice, 'that you and Janna would end up together—especially after you broke my nose for asking her out when we were nineteen.'

'And she was fourteen. I knew you—you couldn't be trusted with her.'

'And you could?' Fergus snorted.

Finn met his eyes at last. 'Aye—I could always be trusted with her—poor fool that I was. Perhaps I should have staked my claim then, before that jerk from Craigmore got hold of her——' He broke off and turned his attention back to his beer.

'Here—you can't bare your soul on that gnat's pee. Have a real drink.'

Finn gave a hollow laugh. 'Who said anything about baring my soul? I'll just drown it instead.'

Fergus disappeared, returning moments later with two whiskies. 'So—tell me about this jerk.'

'Michael? Matthew? I don't know. He hung around her one year—the last summer before she went away. He was there at Christmas, too, but then they moved. He—let's say he made rather more progress than I did.'

Fergus's brow creased in a frown. 'Are you sure? I don't remember seeing much of him with her.'

'That's because you were too busy chasing Lindsay, I expect.'

Fergus grinned. 'Guilty,' he said cheerfully. 'Still, it worked. Look at us now. And what have you got?'

Finn slammed his drink down on the table. 'Nothing. Nothing but memories—and not even them. I can't even remember that summer, it's like a black hole. I keep feeling something happened—something important that I ought to know. I had a car accident—nothing major, but I hit my head. The thing is, Fergus, I don't know what I lost. But I don't really want to remember, because I have a feeling it's something to do with Janna, and why I lost her to Michael or whoever.'

'Why don't you just ask her?'

Finn shrugged. 'I can't. Maybe I don't want to know.'

Fergus was silent for a moment, then shifted his long frame and eyed Finn thoughtfully. 'It's the show next week, on Friday.'

Finn nodded. 'Aye—Janna's birthday. I know.'

'Are you coming?'

He shook his head. 'No. I've got the surgery here.'

Fergus laughed. 'Nobody'll come. They'll all be at the show. Change the day of the surgery.'

Finn rubbed his chin thoughtfully. 'I could—I have the afternoon off the day before. I could shift the surgery to then, and have my afternoon off for the show. I can't manage the morning, though.'

'So you'll have to miss me winning the sheep show.'

'In your dreams,' Finn scoffed. 'John-Alec will win—he always does.'

'No. I'll win. I've got a prize ram this year and some fine lambs. And I'll win the shearing, and tossing the sheaf, and throwing the hammer and the hill-race——'

'Over my dead body!' Finn said calmly. 'You've never beaten me in the hill-race.'

Fergus gave his friend an easy grin. 'But you're out of practice, city-boy. You've gone soft. I'm hard and fit. You don't stand a chance.'

Finn eyed Fergus, assessing the strength of the challenge from his rival. 'I'm more bloody-minded than you,' Finn reminded him. 'I've got staying power.'

'Have you?' Fergus said quietly. 'Then how come I've got Lindsay and you haven't got Janna?'

Finn felt the pain twist deep inside him, and let his breath ease out slowly. 'That was uncalled for,' he whispered harshly. 'Do you no' think I want her?'

'Then have her. Whatever happened with the lad from Craigmore, it was over years ago, Finn. There's been no one else in the year she's been back, and I don't think she'd left anyone behind. Spend the weekend together—turn the clock back.'

'I'm on call. I can't.'

'So switch it. Pay Heather extra. Ask her to cover you, just for tomorrow. It's to be a lovely day again. Why don't you ring Janna in the morning and ask her what she's got planned?'

Finn sighed. The temptation was almost irresistible, but he could see a million pitfalls. 'I expect Heather's got plans for the weekend now.'

'She might not. There's not much goes on in this part of the world, Finn.'

'Janna, then. I expect she's busy. She'll be on this weekend.'

'Amy'll cover her—she's only too glad to earn a bit more. Pay her, as well—damn it, man, what have you got to lose?'

His mind, he could have said. But the idea was so tempting. . .

The phone rang at twelve-thirty. 'Whatever your plans for tomorrow, drop them,' said Fergus. 'I've talked him into getting cover for both of you, and told him to ring you in the morning. Just be available, and take him somewhere that you went during his black hole.'

'Black hole?' Janna said, puzzled.

'That's what he calls his memory loss—the black hole. Janna, he's afraid to look too closely in case he doesn't like what he sees, but he still loves you, I'm sure. Don't let him escape.'

There was a soft click, and the line went dead.

Cradling the receiver carefully, Janna snuggled back down under the quilt. So he still loved her, did he? Then all she had to do was make him remember, and it would be all right.

The best-laid plans of mice and men, and all that, Janna thought. At six that morning, before she had a chance to contact Amy to rearrange her time off, she had a phone call. Some visitors had arrived the previous evening, to a cottage which had Friday change-overs, and one of them had suddenly become terribly breathless. Could she please come? It was really getting very bad.

'Have you got any Ventolin?'

'No—nothing. He's never done this before!'

Janna calmed the panicked woman, and gave her some simple, basic instructions. 'Put him in a warm, damp room with plenty of steam, shut all the windows, and I'll be with you just as soon as I can,' she said, and, gathering up her asthma emergency kit, she rang Finn, told him the venue and raced over to the cottage.

It was inland, on the short stretch of road from Kilbarchan to Inverbeg where it crossed the peninsula, and close to where Fergus had been haymaking the day before. Janna guessed that the still air had been full of dust and pollen, and the man was probably from some relatively dust-free town.

It wasn't the first time it had happened, and she didn't suppose it would be the last.

She arrived to find the man hunched up on the floor in the steamy bathroom, his back against the wall, fighting for breath. There was a shower running, and the bath was full of hot water, but even so his breathing was desperately compromised.

His lips were slightly purple, and he was clutching his chest and gasping desperately.

Janna knelt in front of him. 'Jack? Jack, listen to me. I want you to breathe out as hard as you can, then I'll puff this Ventolin for you and I want you to breathe it in and hold it for as long as you can. Do you understand?'

He nodded, exhaled slightly, and Janna pushed the mouthpiece of the Ventolin inhaler in his mouth and puffed twice as he breathed in. He pushed her hand away, struggling to hold the breath, but he only managed to retain it for a very few seconds before the gasping started again.

'That should help you. I'll give you another dose in a minute. You'll soon start to feel better,' she assured him. She just wished she believed it. He was rapidly going into status asthmaticus, and if Finn didn't arrive soon with the aminophylline injection Janna was very much afraid they would lose him.

'How long's he been like this?' she asked his wife, who was hovering uncertainly behind Janna.

'I don't know. He must have come in here—he opened the window to get more air, I suppose. I shut it when you told me to.'

Janna nodded, rigging up the oxygen mask and placing it over his face. 'OK. Get someone to wait for the doctor—he'll be here in a minute. Then come and sit with your husband and hold his hand—it might calm him. All right, Jack, leave the mask on; it's oxygen. It'll help you—that's it.'

She smoothed back the hair from his brow, noting the pallor and cold, sweaty skin with concern. Damn, he was going down. Where was Finn?

She heard the skid of gravel, the slamming of a door

and Finn's quick tread up the stairs, then he was beside her, taking over with one quick glance.

'Aminophylline,' he muttered, drew it up and inserted the needle into the vein Janna had prepared for him. As the drug slowly entered his system, Janna thought she felt a slight improvement in Jack's tortured breathing.

'That's better,' Finn said, confirming her thoughts. 'Have you given him Ventolin?'

'I tried.'

'Squirt it into the mask—here, I'll do it.'

He puffed the inhaler into the side of the mask, and gradually over the next few minutes the man's colour improved slightly and his breathing became less tormented.

Within fifteen minutes he was much better, but feeling terribly sick.

'I'm sorry, that's the animophylline,' Finn explained. 'How are you feeling otherwise?'

'Still tight,' he muttered. 'I thought my chest was strapped up with steel bands.' He leant his head back, turning so his face was against the cool tiles, and sighed. 'God, I thought I was dying. I really thought I was dying.'

He squeezed his eyes shut and tears oozed between his lids. Finn laid a gentle hand on his shoulder.

'You'll be OK now. I think you could do with going into hospital, just until your breathing's back to normal and the inflammation in your lungs has settled, especially as this is your first attack. If you were used to it I'd let you stay here, but in fact I think you'll be better away from the area for a while because of the haymaking.'

He opened his eyes again. 'Is that what caused it?'

he asked. 'We were watching last night—we went for a walk along the road after we arrrived—and we could see them working till after eight.'

Finn shrugged. 'It seems likely. We don't know, but it's happened before often with visitors. You would have been better with a cottage on the coast.'

'Is there one?' his wife asked. 'I don't really feel we can stay here now, if it's the haymaking that's caused it. We're surrounded by fields.'

'It's worth a try,' Finn said. 'I'll just go and call the ambulance.'

'Ask at the information caravan in Kilbarchan,' Janna told her. 'In fact, the lady who owns this has a couple of little croft-houses down at Port Mackie— that's usually better. It could be worth giving her a ring. Mrs Grainger—do you have the number?'

'I believe so,' the woman said. 'I'll contact her. Perhaps she's got something available—maybe we could swap.'

Finn came back in then. 'They're on their way. They'll take about forty minutes to get here, and then it's two hours to Fort William. It could be worth following the ambulance in the car, if you can do that, because public transport is a bit patchy at this end of the peninsula. It will give you more flexibility. I don't suppose they'll keep him in long—twenty-four hours at most—but you'll want to go with him.'

She nodded. 'Yes, I will. That's a good idea. I must say, we realised it was remote, but I don't think we had any idea how difficult it could be. It must be a very hard life here, with no town close by.'

Janna laughed softly. 'It can be quiet, but really it's beautiful. That's why people stay. Their lives are here. Where else would they go?'

'But you—why are you here? You must have trained elsewhere.'

Janna nodded. 'Aye—Inverness. I hated it. It's a lovely town, but——' she lifted her shoulders in an eloquent shrug '—it's just not home.'

The woman turned to Finn. 'And you? What keeps you here, a young man like you? I would have thought you'd be working in a city hospital, doing a real job.'

Finn chuckled wryly and looked down at her husband on the floor. 'I think your husband would feel I was already doing a real job,' he said gently.

Her hand flew up to her mouth. 'Oh, I'm sorry. I didn't mean to imply that you weren't. Believe me, I'm very, very grateful that you are both here and I think you're doing a wonderful job. I just wondered why—what kept you.'

There was a strange expression on Finn's face. 'There's plenty to keep me here,' he said softly. 'More than enough. It would take something pretty drastic to get me to leave again.'

His eyes locked with Janna's, and for the first time she felt a flicker of hope. Was Fergus right? Did Finn still love her?

Please, God, let it be true. . .

The ambulance came quite quickly, and they settled Jack Tarrent into it and left the house together. Finn walked Janna to her car, then leant against it, rubbing his chin thoughtfully. The rasp of the stubble on his fingertips sent shivers over Janna. She longed to touch it, to feel the rough texture under her own fingertips, to hold him, to tell him how she felt.

She had to wait, though, to play out this charade and hope Finn would remember that long-ago summer, and how their love had blossomed.

She wouldn't think about failure. She must think positively, ask him what he was doing, pursue him as she had done. She took a deep breath.

'Finn——'

'Janna——'

Finn laughed. 'Sorry, you go first.'

She shook her head. 'It was nothing. Go on.'

The stubble scraped again. 'I wondered—— You're probably busy today, on call. I should be, but it looks as if it's going to be a lovely day. I wondered if you wanted to do something—go somewhere.'

The breath eased out of her body on a silent sigh of relief. 'That would be lovely. Actually, I was going to ask you the same. I'm supposed to be on call, but even if I can't get hold of Amy we could still do something if we didn't go too far. I can ring in for messages.'

'So can I, come to that.' A slow, tentative smile curved his lips. 'So, what shall we do?'

'Fishing,' she said instantly. 'Take your bleep. The salmon are leaping, and I just have a fancy for one of MacWhirter's nice, fat fish.'

'Janna,' he admonished with a laugh. 'That's poaching.'

'So?' She met his eyes challengingly. 'You've done it before.'

'Aye—and been tanned for my pains. I'm a respectable member of the community now.'

'Oh, pooh,' she scoffed. 'Don't tell me, Finlay McGregor, that you've turned into a stuffed shirt!'

It was too much. She watched him crumble, the lure of the fish more than he could stand.

'I'll go and change, and pick you up in half an hour. You're a wicked woman.'

She giggled and batted her lashes. 'I try to be,' she teased.

He sucked in his breath, tossed his keys in the air and caught them, then turned away, striding over to his car. 'Be ready.'

'I will,' she said. She climbed into her car and shut the door. 'I am—more than ready. I just hope you are, Finn, because I'm coming to get you.'

CHAPTER NINE

WHILE Finn went to change, Janna quickly phoned Dr MacWhirter at home. 'Bill?' she said. 'It's Janna. I wonder if you could do me a favour? Would you mind if I buy a salmon trout off you, but collect it the unconventional way?'

The old doctor laughed. 'Taking Finn fishing, are you?' he said with a chuckle.

'Yes, and he's got a conscience a mile wide. It would ease mine if I knew it was squared up—and, in fact, he might even ring you himself. If so, pretend you haven't heard from me, OK?'

He agreed, and then added, 'Janna, is everything all right between you and Finn? There was a time, you know, when we all thought—— Well, never mind. I just wondered.'

'I think we'll be OK, Bill. We've had the odd problem, but I think we might make it now.'

He grunted. 'The thing is, lass, if you need anyone to talk to, I'm here.'

She thought of Finn's amnesia. It might be helpful to have a medical opinion if necessary. 'Thanks, Bill, I may well do that. Oh, by the way, can you and Helen come for supper next Friday at my parents'? Check with Helen and let Mum know, could you? I must go—tell me what I owe you for the trout.'

'Nothing, lass—have it, and welcome. Have a lovely day, the two of you. We'll see you on Friday, I expect.'

Janna put the phone down and ran to get ready.

Scruffy old jeans, T-shirt with short sleeves, so they didn't trail in the water, change of clothes because they were bound to get wet, biscuits and a flask of coffee, and waterproofs, because the Highland weather was about as reliable as Mrs Buchan.

Briefly she wondered how the old lady was, but then she heard the unsubtle throb of Finn's engine and, grabbing everything, she ran to the door.

'I'm ready!' she called, checking the answerphone was on then running out, slamming the door behind her.

Finn was sitting in the car, looking reluctant. It was a look she recognised from her childhood. It was only now that she realised it was reluctance and not his usual expression. She felt a twinge of guilt, but buried it. His life would have been boring without her, she thought, and refused to allow herself to acknowledge that he might have liked it that way.

'Got enough junk?' he said drily.

She grinned, refusing to be suppressed. 'I think so. All set?'

'If we must,' he growled softly, and, putting the car in reverse, he turned it round and set off up the road towards MacWhirter's estate.

Once there, they parked the car under some trees so it was nearly invisible, then set off through the damp undergrowth towards the river. 'He'll kill us if he catches us,' Finn grumbled. 'I'll never live it down.'

'Nonsense,' Janna assured him cheerfully, confident on this issue at least. 'He'd love it—think of the fun he'd have. Anyway, I doubt if we'll catch anything. I expect we've lost our touch.'

Finn snorted, and Janna suppressed her grin. There

was nothing like challenging him to get him to do what you wanted. It had always worked, and she thought it probably always would. He just didn't seem to see through it.

Finn led the way, conscious all the time of Janna's quiet tread behind him. He had taught her how to walk softly through woodland, and it was fascinating to him now to listen to her.

He smiled slightly. She hadn't forgotten how to move—and she hadn't forgotten how to tickle trout, either, he'd stake his life on it. She was just winding him up, throwing down the gauntlet.

Well, he'd humour her by picking it up. He'd cleared it with MacWhirter anyway, before leaving. Funny, he hadn't seemed surprised—more amused. Everyone always found Janna's antics amusing, and they had never caused any real harm.

Until the last, with the lad from Craigmore. That prank had lost its edge, he thought sadly. Poor lass, getting pregnant and being dumped like that by the louse—and then not being able to contact Finn when she had needed a friend to talk to about it.

He wasn't sure how much use he would have been. Even now he was still angry. Still, it was over. According to Fergus there was no one else. Perhaps it was time to move—if only he could be sure of her.

He felt a slight tug on his shirt and stopped.

She gestured slightly with her head, her eyes alight, and as he followed her gaze he saw a doe with a fawn, still speckled on its back, grazing quietly not thirty feet away.

They stood motionless, watching, until with a sudden slight shift of the wind the doe caught their scent and raised her head in alarm. Instantly she saw them and bounded away, her fawn at her heels.

Finn let his breath out slowly and turned to Janna. 'Beautiful. It's a shame they're such a pest.'

She laughed. 'The venison butchers and deer-hunters wouldn't agree with you. Come on, my fingers are itching.'

So were Finn's, but not to tickle trout. He wanted to run his hands through the dark mass of Janna's hair, holding her by it and drawing her up against him. . .

'Come on!' She gave him a little push, and he started forward again, towards the deep, quiet pool where he had first kissed her.

Damn, this was going to be difficult. He was determined not to touch her, because he was finding his control more ragged with every day, and he wouldn't make love to her until he was sure she loved him back, and wasn't just replaying their childhood for fun.

He hoped to God she wasn't, because it was even harder now than it had been then, and if she was just playing it would tear him to shreds.

They reached the pool, and Janna set down her things and turned to him. 'Look at them! You can see the water heaving with them!'

They sat on the bank for a while, eating biscuits, watching the fish slip silently through the water, gathering their strength for the next part of their final journey upstream.

Then Finn stripped off his shirt, laid it on the bank and lay down, sliding his arm into the cold, still water without leaving so much as a ripple. Good, he hadn't lost his touch.

'I'll race you,' he said softly.

'You're on.' Janna lay down a little further

upstream, eased her hand into the chilly water and winked at him.

'The winner gets a kiss,' she said with a provocative smile. Finn was suddenly very glad he was lying flat on his front, because his body had reacted immediately to the promise in those wonderful grey-green eyes.

He felt the slight movement of the water, then something nibbling at his fingertips. Slowly, so slowly, he ran one finger under its chin, then back, down the belly, until the fish was lying in his hand, mesmerised by the rhythmic movements of his fingers.

Then, with a quick flick of the wrist and a roll, he flipped the fish out on to the bank and sat up, grinning. 'I won,' he announced proudly, feeling positively adolescent all over again.

Janna rolled on to her back, sat up and studied him.

'It seems a shame, really, to kill it,' she said thoughtfully.

Finn looked at it, then gently, without damaging its scales, he picked it up and slid it back into the water. With a flick of its tail it was gone.

Finn raised his head. 'Do I still get a kiss?'

'Oh, yes—that's part of the fun,' Janna said softly. She patted the mossy ground by her side, and with his heart pounding like a steam-hammer Finn moved up beside her.

'Now what?' he said.

'Now I kiss you.' She reached up and pulled him down until he was lying in the soft mossy bed, and then unbearably slowly she leant over him, threading her hands through his hair and tantalising him with the promise of her lips. 'Close your eyes,' she murmured, and with a shuddering sigh he let his lids fall.

'You're playing with fire,' he whispered hoarsely.

'Mmm.'

And then her lips met his, and heat exploded in his body like a wild thing. He reached for her, but she pinned his arms down, tutting at him and shackling his wrists above his head so he was helpless.

He wasn't, of course. He could easily have overpowered her, but he chose not to. Instead he lay there and endured the torment of her teasing, tantalising mouth as she sipped and brushed and nibbled until he was almost out of his mind. Then with a ragged groan he rolled her on to her back and followed her, cupping her head in his hands and kissing her until she sobbed with need.

Then slowly, reluctantly, he let her go, lifting himself away to lie beside her, facing her, their eyes locked as their breathing slowly steadied.

'You kiss like a fallen angel,' he murmured gruffly.

She smiled. 'You taught me.'

His lips quirked in an involuntary smile. 'It's a shame I didn't teach you to drive so well.'

Guilt clouded her eyes. 'I meant to ask you for the bill—I haven't paid you for the lights.'

'Forget it,' he told her. 'It was my fault, I didn't give you room.'

Her hand came out and cupped his cheek tenderly. 'You're a lousy liar, Finn McGregor,' she whispered. Then she got to her feet, picked up their things and turned back. 'Are you still sitting there?'

'I thought you wanted to catch a trout.'

She smiled. 'Did you? I wonder what gave you that idea.'

'We could cook it on the beach—wrap it in foil and light a fire with driftwood.'

She seemed to go suddenly still. 'That sounds—wonderful. Is the race still on?'

'What do you think?'

He watched as she dropped her things and lay down again, her arm entering the water as smoothly as his. He'd taught her well, as his father had taught him. He lay down again and slid his arm back into the water. It took longer this time, probably because his mind was on Janna and that mind-bending kiss, and not on the fish itself.

Just when he was getting somewhere there was a great splash, a shriek of delight, and Janna landed one, dispatched it with a stone and put it into a plastic bag.

'I won,' she said with a cheeky grin.

Finn snorted. 'Well, you aren't having another kiss, you brazen hussy. Come on, little minx, out of here before we get caught.'

Giggling like kids, they ran back through the wood, startling another deer so that it bounded away from them in panic.

Once back at the car they climbed inside, hid the fish under a seat and grinned at each other. 'Coffee?' Janna said.

'Good idea. Where?'

'Here—I've got a flask.'

'Lord, woman, is there anything you haven't brought?'

She chuckled and handed him a cup of coffee. 'Drink up, we ought to go and check my phone.'

The light on the answerphone was winking when they got in. Janna turned it on and they both listened.

'Hello, it's Sue here, from the pub. I've got a rider who's fallen off one of the ponies out on a ride and seems to have a rather painful arm, possibly broken. I wonder if you could pop over when you're back, Janna. Thanks.'

Janna turned off the answerphone. 'Should I go, or will you?'

Finn shrugged. 'It's lunchtime—we'll both go, and we can grab a bite. Anyway, if it's a fracture you'll need me, so I might as well come.'

He took his bag and they set off, crossing the road and walking the fifty yards up the road to the pub. They found the patient sitting outside under a tree, her arm held very awkwardly against her side. She was supporting it with the other arm, and leaning on a man who was probably her husband. Sue was standing nearby, and two children were looking on worriedly.

'Looks like a collarbone or shoulder,' Janna said to Finn, assessing the appearance of the limb as they crossed the grass.

'Mmm. Getting the shirt off could be tricky. Scissors job, I fancy. Hi, there. I'm Dr McGregor and this is Sister Murray. I assume you're our patient?'

The woman smiled thinly. 'Afraid so. The pony shied and my seat isn't what it was. I thought ponytrekking would be fun, but perhaps I should have taken up flying instead,' she added with a weary chuckle.

Finn laughed. 'Oh, dear. Well, let's have a look at you—do you mind if we go inside? I'd like to take your shirt off to have a closer look.'

'No, that's fine. I was sitting out here because of the fresh air,' she explained. 'I felt suddenly queasy.'

They helped her inside, accompanied by the entourage, and Finn produced a pair of scissors and apologised for wrecking her shirt.

'Oh, forget it. I couldn't possibly struggle out of it,' she told them.

Once the shirt was all snipped away it was easy to see what was wrong. The top of her humerus had dropped down and in towards her chest, because the head of it had dislocated from the shoulder joint.

'Ouch,' Finn said softly. 'Well, you've dislocated your shoulder, I'm afraid. I want to check for any nerve damage or anything that could indicate another site of injury. How does your hand feel?'

'Sort of numb,' she told him, 'and cotton woolly. Pins and needles, a bit. My fingers are cold.'

Finn felt for her radial pulse, and pursed his lips. 'I think you might have trapped the brachial artery, got a kink in it or something, because your pulse is rather weak here. How long ago did you fall?'

Her husband looked at his watch. 'About an hour. It took us ages to get back.'

Finn nodded, checking for nerve damage and temperature over the whole limb. 'Right, I don't think I should leave it too long before it's reduced. I don't want you to have to go all the way to hospital like that, without any decent circulation to your arm. The nerves seem all right, and I don't think you've got any other fractures, but I'd still like you to go in and have it checked, even if it seems all right afterwards. It will just make the journey less painful if we can get it back, but primarily I want that circulation restored.'

He turned to Janna. 'I think the best thing would be to take her back to the surgery, give her some pethidine and reduce it there.'

She nodded. 'Fine. Shall I go and get the room ready?'

'Good idea. We'll be over in a minute.'

Janna went back across to her house, picked up their things from the hall floor and took them to the kitchen. The fish she laid in the sink, ready for cooking on the beach that night.

Did he remember that they had done that before? she wondered as she prepared the consulting-room for their patient. It had been down at Camas Ciuicharan, on the sand, and afterwards they had stayed there until the tide came in and put the fire out with a hiss of steam, leaving them in the darkness.

The fish had tasted wonderful, she remembered. Would it taste so good tonight?

She hoped so. Why had he suggested it? Of course, it hadn't been the only time they had done it, but that time had been particularly special. Fergus and Lindsay had been with them, she remembered, and Fergus had been so busy keeping Lindsay occupied that she had had Finn to herself. Really, to get the right effect, they should repeat the evening exactly.

As soon as she was finished in the room, she rang them. 'Can you get a babysitter and join us on the beach tonight to cook a fish?' she asked Lindsay.

'Do you want us?'

'Yes—you were there before.'

'Oh—right. Fine. What time?'

'Eight—and bring a bottle of dry white wine.'

She hung up, went and checked the room and opened the front door just as Finn and the woman's husband arrived. Sue, apparently, was taking the children to feed the ponies.

Finn gave the woman some intravenous pethidine to relax her, laid her face-down on the examination couch and slowly, very gently, let her arm hang.

'Ow—oh, it hurts,' she breathed, biting her lip, and

Finn rubbed her back gently to free the muscles. Then, rotating the arm outwards, he gave a careful jerk and the end of the humerus slipped back with a little click.

She gave a gasp, sighed with relief, and then Finn sat her up, supporting her arm, while Janna strapped it firmly to her chest to support it.

Within moments the colour was returning to her fingers and her pulse was restored, with the inevitable pins and needles.

'Excellent,' Finn said in satisfaction. Had Janna imagined it, or had he sighed with relief? Very likely. Fractures could be an unseen complication of dislocations, and Janna imagined he didn't want to be hauled up before the Medical Defence Union for malpractice! She knew that if the circulation hadn't been compromised he wouldn't have touched the dislocation with a barge-pole, and no doubt his notes would reflect that fact.

'Right, I'll do a letter for you to take with you, then you need to go to Casualty at Fort William and get it X-rayed and checked over properly. OK?'

While her husband went to collect the car and the children, Janna helped the woman put her cardigan back on over the top and button it to give her some respectability, and then Finn handed them the letter and watched them go.

This time Janna couldn't mistake the relief in his eyes. 'Thank God that went as well as it did. I hate reducing fractures without radiological backup, but with her artery compressed it would have been more negligent to leave it than to try and reduce it.'

'Absolutely,' she replied. 'Did I hear you say something about lunch?'

He grinned, that toe-curling, mind-bendingly sexy

grin of his. 'I wondered how long it would be before you remembered your stomach.'

'Oh, talking of stomachs,' she said as they headed for the pub, 'Fergus and Lindsay are joining us tonight on the beach.'

'Just like old times,' he said softly.

Janna hoped it would be exactly like old times—or one of them in particular.

The tide was way out, playing right into her hands. Finn and Fergus laid the fire and lit it while Janna prepared the fish and Lindsay fed the baby.

'That's something that isn't quite the same,' Lindsay said quietly to Janna. 'There were only four of us before. Now there are five—seven, if you count the two at home.' She was sitting in the car, and Janna was working on a rock close by. She looked up from the fish and smiled at her friend.

'I think you should.' Her eyes flicked to the baby. 'It's really been quite a while, hasn't it?'

Lindsay smoothed the fine, soft hair of her baby's head and stared down at her, and the expression on her face made Janna's heart ache. She looked away, but not before Lindsay had seen.

'Janna, it'll be your turn soon.'

'I hope you're right,' she said quietly, without conviction.

'Has he mentioned anything yet? Anything about the past?'

'Yes, lots,' Janna told her. 'But unfortunately nothing about the particular bit I'm interested in.'

'Maybe you should tell him? You know, say, "We did this together, in the summer you've forgotten." Things like that, just to jog him.'

Janna shrugged. 'I don't know. I don't know enough about the treatment of amnesia. I'll play it by ear.'

She wrapped the fish in thick layers of soaked newspaper, laid it on the rock and looked down towards Finn and Fergus. 'They've got the fire going nicely—you ought to move down there with the baby, keep the midges off.'

'There aren't many here, that's the beauty of this spot. The barn roof isn't on yet, I see.'

They exchanged a grin. 'Has Fergus got hold of Angus yet?'

'Uh-huh. He starts on Monday.'

'Finn will be livid.'

'Yup.'

They chuckled.

The sunset was spectacular.

Lindsay and Fergus were on the beach beside the fire, stretched out on a rug, with Lindsay's head pillowed on Fergus's hip. He was leaning back on one elbow, the other hand idly toying with Lindsay's hair, staring down at her with a tender expression on his face. The baby was asleep in the car, and they were making the most of a quiet moment.

Finn turned to Janna with a smile that didn't quite reach his eyes. 'It's nauseating. Let's leave these two lovebirds alone for a while and go for a stroll.'

They walked out along the beach until they reached the incoming tide, then climbed up on to the rocks and followed the waterline round the point, towards where they had found little Sophie. Even now Janna found it hard to realise how close they had come to losing her.

'They went home today, I imagine,' Finn said, staring at the spot. 'They were lucky to be taking her home alive after that little stunt.'

'Don't,' Janna said, a shiver running over her, and Finn pulled her into his side and wrapped his arm round her shoulders, holding her there against his warmth as they strolled along the rocks.

It was quiet, the water almost motionless, and suddenly they heard the eerie call of a seal.

'Listen,' Janna said, turning her head slightly.

They stood still, conscious only of the cries of the seals, the quiet lap of the waves and each other.

Slowly, as if afraid to break the spell, Finn bent his head and touched his lips to hers. 'Janna,' he breathed, the word almost lost in the quiet of the evening, then he drew her into his arms and rested his chin on her head, holding her so she could hear the steady rhythm of his heart.

'I've missed you,' he murmured after a while. 'It seems so long since we've been together without some antagonism between us. I wish I could understand it.'

Her heart speeded up. 'It's all part of what you've lost,' she told him, her voice gentle. 'Maybe one day something will trigger it and it will all come back.'

He eased her away and looked down into her eyes; the last rays of the sun were blinding her, so she couldn't read his expression. 'Janna,' he asked carefully, 'did something happen that summer—something that hurt you and caused this rift between us? Something I ought to remember?'

'No, nothing that hurt me, but something I need you to remember, if you can.'

He gazed out to sea, his eyes troubled. 'You're hurt because of me, aren't you?' he said at last.

She slid her hand into his, meshing their fingers. 'In a way. It's not your fault; I know that now.'

'If I never remember—will it matter?'

She shook her head. 'No. I'll tell you, in the end. It's just how to do it.'

'We've been here before, like this, haven't we? With Fergus and Lindsay, and the seals—eating MacWhirter's stolen trout in the sunset.' He turned to her again. 'Is that what this is all about, Janna? Memory Lane?'

She nodded, chewing her lip. Please God, let it be working. 'Do you remember?' she asked tentatively.

'Bits—little snatches. You wore a blue dress.'

She nodded again. 'Fergus and Lindsay were totally taken up with each other, and we went for a walk, just like tonight.'

'And I kissed you.'

'Yes.'

He sighed. 'There was more, wasn't there?'

'Not that night.'

'Your birthday party, then. I don't remember any of it.'

'I've got a video,' she offered. 'Someone filmed it.'

'I'd like to see it—I think.'

She stood on tiptoe and kissed his chin. 'I'll let you have it. Come on, we ought to go back. Fergus and Lindsay will be worried.'

They turned, surprised to find that the tide had come in quite a distance and was now lapping over the edge of the fire, making the logs hiss.

Fergus and Lindsay had packed up their things and were ready to go.

'Thanks for coming,' Janna said with a faint smile.

'Our pleasure,' Fergus replied.

Finn said nothing, watching until they had gone,

then he turned back to check the fire was out. 'All set?' he asked her.

She nodded. They drove back to her house in a thoughtful silence. Finn didn't stop. He seemed preoccupied, and Janna guessed he wanted to think about their conversation. She hoped she wasn't doing the wrong thing, trying to trigger his memory. She didn't think she was, but it worried her just the same. Still, it was their only chance.

She watched him go, then closed the curtains, curled up on the sofa and picked up the phone.

'Mum? About Friday—— Oh, Helen's been on the phone, has she? Damn. Well, let me explain. . .'

Janna found the suspense of that week crippling. The stage was set for Friday. Bill and Helen, Fergus and Lindsay and a few other couples of her parents' age were coming over for drinks after the Kilbarchan Show. That came first, of course, and Janna wondered if it would trigger anything, or if Finn had been to so many that one more would be neither here nor there.

The week was a busy one. Betty Buchan was discharged from hospital on Thursday, weak, confused and quite unable to care for herself.

Janna was furious, and spent a long time on the phone to the hospital and to Social Services, trying to sort something out. In the end she rang Finn.

'Betty Buchan's home without any support, totally institutionalised, and can't understand why there's no bell to call the nurse when she wants something. I can't leave her here, Finn. She's not safe.'

'I'm coming over later,' he said. 'Give me a while, I'll make a few calls and be with you. I'm doing the surgery at Kilbarchan this afternoon, anyway. Can you get a neighbour in for a while so you can get on?'

'I'll try. I'll ring you again if not.'

There was no one, so she called him back. 'You'll have to sort it out now, Finn. Please.'

He arrived a little while later, took one look at Betty and sighed. 'Why is she home? It's cruel.' He pulled up a chair beside her, huddled into her old rocker, a terrified expression on her face.

'Hello, there, Betty. How are you feeling?'

'Who are you?' she quavered, clearly all at sea. 'I don't know where I am—where am I?'

'You're back home, my love,' he said gently, holding her hands. 'Don't you remember it?'

She shook her head. 'Where's the wee nurse gone? She looked a'ter me—where am I?'

'You're hame, sweetheart—back in your ain wee hoos,' Finn soothed, the brogue heavy in his voice as he tried to reassure her.

It didn't work. She looked round blankly. 'I've never been here—I don't know where I am. I'm afeared. . .'

Finn patted her hands, stood up and turned to Janna, his face black. 'What were they thinking of, sending her out like this?' he growled.

'Apparently her family said she'd be all right, they'd look after her,' Janna told him drily.

He snorted. 'So where are they?'

Janna gave a short laugh. 'They're all busy. They might pop in tomorrow.'

'Right, that's it,' he said firmly. 'I've messed around long enough, and nearly cost her her life. Enough's enough.'

He called the nursing home in Craigmore, confirmed that he was admitting her immediately, and called the ambulance.

'They'll be thrilled, they've only just brought her back,' Janna pointed out.

'Tough,' he growled. 'That's what the service is there for. They'll be here in an hour—can you pack her some things and stay with her?'

Janna laughed. 'Do I have a choice?'

The smile softened his face a little. 'I don't think so. I'm sorry. It makes me so cross.'

'Me too. Yes, I'll stay with her and sort her out.'

'Good. I'll see you back at the surgery as soon as you can.'

She nodded. 'OK. Oh, and Finn? I meant to ask you, you haven't forgotten tomorrow night? The little get-together at my parents' house?'

'Another trip down Memory Lane?' he said wryly. 'Don't worry, Janna, I wouldn't miss it for the world.'

After the ambulance had gone Janna went down to Port Mackie to see their asthma patient. He had moved from the cottage inland to one next to Mrs Grainger on the beach at Port Mackie, and Janna just wanted to check that he was well and happy with his treatment. He had been sent out on Ventolin, and Janna had been asked to keep an eye on him.

She arrived at the house to find they were just clearing away lunch and making coffee.

'Join us,' they suggested. She was desperately tempted, but declined. She really needed to get on back to the surgery, to help Finn with the patients.

'How is your chest now, Jack?' she asked him, checking his respiratory capacity with the peak flow meter. 'It looks very good, actually.'

'Oh, it is; it's much better. We haven't dared stray away from the beach, mind you! It seems to be the long grasses—we live in a town, and all the grass is mown long before it flowers!'

'You'll have to avoid the haymaking season in future, then. Come earlier or later.'

'We will. We want to come back—it's so peaceful and beautiful here we can hardly believe it. We went for a walk round the headland yesterday—there's a cove there with a ruined barn—looks like someone's doing it up. Shame, I would have liked to have bought it and converted it into a house.'

You and a million others, Janna thought wryly, including me. 'It belongs to Dr McGregor,' she told them. 'He's going to live there when it's done up.'

'Lucky man.'

And hopefully, Janna thought, I'm going to live there with him.

Making her farewells, she went back to the surgery and tried to concentrate on her patients, but her mind was on Finn in his consulting-room, his soft, deep voice penetrating her thoughts with startling ease.

Oh, please, God, she thought for the thousandth time, give him back to me. . .

CHAPTER TEN

JANNA's birthday dawned bright, clear and beautifully warm—just as it had for the show seven years ago. That show hadn't been on her birthday, but on the day before, and she had teased Finn mercilessly. She rattled through her visits that morning, the last one being to Jessie, Finn's mother.

'Hello, dear! What are you doing here? Happy birthday!'

'Oh, Jessie, you remembered!'

The elderly lady chuckled. 'Difficult not to—it's all Finn's talked about for days. You know, lass, I've missed you,' Jessie told her. 'I know Finn thought he'd save you the bother of doing my leg, but to be honest, Janna, I used to look forward to you coming in.'

Janna laughed and hugged her. 'I looked forward to it, too. Hopefully I'll be seeing a lot more of you again.'

Jessie studied her. 'He still loves you, you know.'

Janna was still. 'Yes, I believe he does,' she said with quiet conviction. 'That's just as well, because I don't intend to let him get away again. Now, let's see this leg of yours—has he been looking after it properly?'

'Och, aye—it's started to heal at last. Finn says it must be his magic touch.'

Janna laughed. 'Don't spoil his fun, but it had started to heal when I last saw it.'

She checked the dressing, but it wasn't yet ready to

change. She could see the margins of the ulcer were
starting to close in, however. It was looking good. 'I'll
do it on Monday,' she told Jessie.

'Will he let you?'

'By Monday? He'll be putty in my hands, Jessie.'

Finn's mother chuckled. 'He always was, Janna—
he always was.'

Janna hoped their faith was justified.

'So your ram won, eh? Wonders will never cease.'

Fergus ignored his friend's good-natured ribbing. He
was too disgustingly pleased with himself to retaliate.

'Are you ready for the hill-run?' he said instead.

'Of course. Are you?'

'Aye. And tossing the sheaf. That was always
mine—except the once.'

Finn looked at him. 'I won it?'

'Uh-huh. The last time you entered it.'

'Seven years ago.'

Fergus rested a large, reassuring hand on Finn's
shoulder. 'Don't worry. It'll come.'

Finn shook his head. 'I doubt it, after so many years.
Long-term loss is usually permanent.'

'We'll see. And don't imagine I'll feel sorry for you
and give you an advantage.'

Finn chuckled. 'Fergus, I never supposed
you would.'

Just then the tannoy spluttered to life. 'Entrants for
tossing the sheaf, please go to the top corner of
the field.'

'That's us,' Fergus said, throwing his arm round
Finn's shoulders. 'Come on, old man, let's see what
you're made of now.'

*   *   *

Janna stood by the top corner of the field, watching all the contestants facing up to each other. There was a lot of good-natured ribbing, and she noticed a few visitors joining in. They wouldn't stand a chance, of course, not against this lot. There was a lot of pride at stake.

It was a strange, traditional contest. Two extending ladders were standing up about fifteen feet apart, rearing up into the sky and supported by guy lines, and slung between them was a horizontal pole which was steadily raised. The idea was to pitch a sack stuffed with straw—the sheaf—over the pole. The man who cleared the greatest height was the winner, and Finn and Fergus had always been neck and neck, Fergus winning by a short head. Except that once, when Finn had won.

She watched as the contest started, Lindsay beside her with the two younger children in a buggy and the oldest holding her hand.

As the pole rose, so the visitors and other weaker contenders were knocked out. At last it was just Finn and Fergus.

Janna, her heart pounding, remembered the year Finn had won, and what she had said in these closing stages of the competition. Loudly, clearly, so there could be no mistake, she called out, 'The winner gets a kiss, remember.'

Finn turned, their eyes locked for an age, then he turned back to Fergus. 'Stand by to lose your crown, old friend,' he advised with a half-smile.

Fergus laughed. 'No way.'

'Fergus Baird, you're a married man,' Lindsay warned.

There was a lot of good-natured laughter, then

Fergus picked up the pitchfork. They both cleared the pole at that height, and the next, but the next time Fergus's sheaf caught the pole, wobbled and fell back.

Finn smirked.

'Best of three, remember,' Fergus told him, and handed him the pitchfork.

Finn's pitch sailed over the pole.

So did Fergus's second.

Finn's second hit it and fell back.

They had one clear each. It was all down to the last.

Fergus went first again, but the sheaf hit the pole and dropped back on the wrong side.

Janna's hands were damp. 'Please, please win,' she whispered.

Finn stabbed the fork into the sheaf, hefted it, and Janna saw his muscles bunch and heave as he threw the sheaf high in the air.

It cleared the pole with feet to spare, and Janna threw herself into his arms, laughing with relief, and, grabbing his head in her hands, she pulled it down for a blistering kiss.

The crowd went mad.

'You're in public, children,' Fergus said softly beside them, and Finn raised his head with reluctance to meet Fergus's eyes, a victor's smile on his face.

'I beat you.'

Fergus grinned ruefully. 'I had noticed. Congratulations. Of course,' he added casually, 'there's always the hill-race.'

'Does the winner of that get a kiss, too?' Finn asked Janna softly.

'At least,' Janna promised.

Finn's eyes burned into hers. 'Right. I'd better go and eat a bar of chocolate.'

She grinned. 'I'm ahead of you.' She handed him a huge bar, and he laughed.

'You must really want me to win.'

Her eyes said it all.

The hill-race was later on, and as Janna and Lindsay watched them set off Janna found her nerves were jangling. If all went well, she would take Finn tonight down to the barn, and rerun the last reel of Finn's missing link.

She was terrified. What if it didn't work? What if he didn't remember? She felt sick with anticipation, and would have gone to pieces without Lindsay's quiet support.

'It'll be fine,' she murmured. 'Don't worry.'

'I hope you're right. I'm almost a basket-case.'

They watched the runners on the hill, tiny dots above the village, and then they turned and started on the home run.

The crowd moved back to the gate, lining the road, cameras at the ready, and then they came into view, Finn and Fergus leading, miles ahead of the rest, their long legs pounding down the road and eating up the last few hundred yards.

They were side by side, grim determination on both their faces, but as they reached the line Finn threw himself forward and breasted the tape a fraction ahead.

Both men floundered to a halt, standing with their hands on their knees, gasping for air for a moment, then Fergus sat down and laughed up at Finn.

'Bastard,' he said cheerfully, still breathless. 'I nearly had you.'

Finn straightened and grinned. 'But not quite. You're right, though, I'm out of practice.' He turned to Janna, the grin widening. 'How about that kiss?'

She laughed and backed away. 'Later—you can wash first. You're wringing wet. I'll see you at my parents'.'

Something altered in his smile. Good lord, she thought, he's nervous too. Somehow that made her feel much better.

Finn stood in the kitchen, staring out of the window into the gathering gloom. Something was going to happen tonight, he knew. He'd watched the video of Janna's party, and seeing himself in it was like watching a stranger. Yet tonight he would find out what had happened.

He closed his eyes, hearing again his father's voice. 'Hiding from things doesn't change them, son. They're still there. It's better to face them.'

He heard Janna's footsteps behind him. 'Here you are—I've been looking for you. I want you to dance with me.'

He turned, smiling gently down at her. She looked scared, too—as scared as he felt.

'Come on, then,' he murmured and, taking her hand, he led her into the dining-room. The furniture had been cleared out of the way, and the French doors were open into the garden. The lights were low, and Fergus and Lindsay were linked together, swaying slowly to the music.

Finn drew Janna into his arms, noticing with detachment how well she fitted under his chin, her arms snug round his waist, her soft breasts pressing gently against his ribs. He could hardly bear to move, because every brush of her thighs against his heated his blood to fever-pitch.

She sighed softly, inching closer, their legs meshing

so that her thigh chafed against the hard, throbbing ache she had caused.

'Dammit, Janna,' he growled under his breath.

Her soft laughter rippling round him, she guided him out through the French doors into the dusky garden.

'I owe you a kiss,' she breathed and, lifting trembling hands, she cupped his face and brought it down to her lips.

Fire shot through him. With a startled groan he dragged her up against him and plundered her mouth, seeking to put out the fire and yet only seeming to fan the flames.

She eased away, reaching out a hand to him. 'Come on. They don't need us.'

He trailed behind her, bemused. 'Where are we going?'

'The bay.'

'Now?'

'Uh-huh. Get in.'

He realised they were standing beside her father's car. 'Shouldn't we take mine?'

She shook her head. 'No. Come on.'

He got in. Was this it? Part of the past? He leant his head back against the leather head-rest of the Jaguar and sighed raggedly. What had happened?

She drove too fast. She always had—and it wasn't his fault. He had taught her well, but not even he could eliminate that streak of recklessness that ran through her.

They turned off the road and pulled up beside the barn. Cutting the engine, she climbed out and went to the boot, pulling out a blanket.

'Come on.'

He unfolded himself from the car, following her

cautiously. His mind was scrambled, watching her
sway away from him in that soft, pale dress.

She wore it always, in the dream.

She turned in the doorway and beckoned to him,
and, helpless, he followed.

She was sitting on the rug, spread out in front of
the opening, with the bay in front of them and the
stars above—just like the dream.

'Janna——'

She touched her finger to her lips, patting the rug
beside her. He shrugged off his jacket, folded it as a
pillow, then lay down beside her.

Then her lips brushed his, and he was lost.

The kiss was endless, her hands moving over him,
tormenting him, undoing buttons and easing his shirt
aside, her fingers cool against his fevered skin.

He wanted her. He had wanted her for years, more
years than he could bear to remember, and he couldn't
hold back any more.

Hands shaking, he stripped off his clothes and turned
to her, watching spellbound as she lifted the dress over
her head and cast it aside.

She was naked under it—just like the dream.

'Finn—make love to me,' she whispered unsteadily,
and, reaching for her, he drew her into his arms.

Lord, she felt so sweet! So right, so exactly as she
did in the dream. Soft, warm, yielding, her body sinu-
ous yet womanly. He wanted to bury himself inside
her, hold her, kiss her.

He would probably regret it, but just this once he
needed it all. His hands caressed her, revelling in the
soft, smooth skin, so warm and silky, smelling of
flowers and rainwater and something else—something
basic and womanly that snapped his control and

unleashed the elemental man in him.

He moved over her, gritting his teeth as her legs wound round him, drawing him down towards her.

'Easy,' he muttered, but she wouldn't slow down, drawing him in relentlessly.

He thought he would die.

Unable to move, he rested his head against her shoulder and struggled for control. Beneath him she shifted restlessly, and he kissed her, soothing her.

'Steady, Janna,' he murmured. 'Take it nice and slow.'

'No,' she sobbed. Her hands clutched at him, pleading. 'Finn, please—now!'

His body racked with shudders, he held back a second longer, then surrendered, driving into her with long, deep strokes, matching her rhythm until suddenly, without warning, she cried out, convulsing beneath him.

The savage cry was torn from his lungs, flung clear across the bay to shatter into echoes against the distant islands.

Then the realisation hit him.

It wasn't a dream at all.

It was a memory.

Janna lay beneath him, her hands tenderly smoothing the sweat-slicked skin of his back as his heaving chest slowed and his head lay cradled on her shoulder.

'Janna?' he murmured.

'Mmm.'

'I love you.'

Tears sprang to her eyes. 'Oh, Finn—oh, darling, I love you too, so much——'

She broke off, biting her lip to hold back the

tears, and he lifted his head and stared deep into her eyes.

'I thought it was a dream. All this——' He waved his arm around, gesturing at the barn. 'Every night, I dream I'm here with you, like this, and it's all—— Was this an action replay?'

She nodded. 'As near as I could make it.'

He gave a short laugh. 'Let me tell you, it's pretty damn close.' He swallowed. 'Oh, love, what happened to us?' he whispered, his voice cracking. 'I knew I'd lost something, but I never realised how much.'

She cupped his jaw, soothing him, and he turned his face into her hand and pressed a kiss to her palm.

'Then I went away, had the accident and you didn't hear from me. Is that why——?' He hesitated, then started again. 'Is that why you had an affair with Michael?'

She was stunned. 'Michael? Who's Michael?'

'The lad from Craigmore. You know.'

'Matthew?' she said blankly. 'I didn't have an affair with Matthew. What are you talking about?'

'But the baby——' He floundered to a halt, his face in the moonlight registering shock. 'Dear God,' he whispered. 'The baby was mine. . . Oh, Janna, love, no.'

He gathered her into his arms, cradling her tenderly against his chest, his cheek against hers. For a long moment they lay there without moving, then finally he lifted his head, kissing their tears from her cheeks, and stared deep into her eyes. 'What did you go through without me? Dear God, darling, you must have thought I didn't care—— Oh, Janna, love, I'm sorry. . .'

'I needed you,' she whispered brokenly. 'One minute

you wanted to marry me, the next you wouldn't even return my calls. I thought my father had talked you out of it.'

'Talked me out of what? When?'

'When you spoke to him. We left here, full of plans to marry straight away, and you took me back to the house and collared my father. You went in the study with him and you were there for ages, then when you came out you told me he'd talked a lot of sense, and we should wait until you were qualified and I'd done my basic training before we got married——'

'Hang on. Are you telling me I asked your father if I could marry you?'

Janna stared at him. Oh, God. He had only remembered their lovemaking, not the loving that had gone with it.

He eased away from her, sitting up, one leg bent and his arms wrapped round his knee, staring out over the sea.

'We were going to get married?'

His voice sounded rough, unused, and Janna felt dread clawing at her throat. She knelt up beside him, watching him.

'Finn, if you don't feel like that about me any more I'll quite understand. I probably bulldozed you— everyone keeps telling me I always bulldozed you into everything—and I never meant you to do anything you didn't want——'

He turned, his face tender in the moonlight. 'Bulldozed? Janna, you never bulldozed me into anything. I was always more than willing.'

She dropped her eyes, staring at her hands. 'That's not true. I used to bully you.'

He started to laugh, his shoulders shaking, and

Janna, her emotions strung to breaking point, felt tears well in her eyes.

'Don't laugh at me!' she whispered raggedly. 'I'm trying to be honest with you. It's hard enough——'

Suddenly she was in his arms, lying across his lap with her face held between his hands, and all laughter was gone from his eyes.

'Janna, I'm not laughing at you. It's just the idea of you bullying me. I knew full well what you were doing. I let you get away with it because I wanted to, but never think for a moment that you pushed me into anything against my will. Against my better judgement, certainly, but only because of the wild streak in me that you only ever found. As for changing my mind about you, I hardly think so. I've loved you for twenty-five years, sweetheart. I'm not about to stop now.'

She stared up at his beloved face, and gradually the truth of his words sank in. She smiled—a soft, siren's smile.

'What do you say we get dressed, go back to my house and do this all over again, but somewhere comfortable?'

He chuckled. 'It would have been more comfortable here, only someone hijacked my builder.'

She wriggled guiltily. 'Um—it was in a good cause. He was about to put the roof on, and I needed the stars above us.'

Finn laughed softly. 'I hope Angus doesn't know why.'

'No—I'm afraid Fergus and Lindsay do, but no one else.'

'Hmm.' He reached behind and passed her her dress. 'Here, hussy, put this on. We'll go back to your house, get you properly dressed and then go back to your parents. I think it's time I had another conversation with your father.'

'Are you going to be boring?' she said with a mock pout.

'Absolutely. Come on. I'm beginning to feel a bit exposed here.'

They dressed hastily, and as he picked up his jacket something caught his eye. 'Oh, I forgot. I've got a birthday present for you. Here.'

He handed her an envelope, creased where their heads had lain on it in his jacket, and she slit it open and pulled out the contents.

'It's too dark. I can't really see. What is it?'

'The deeds of this place. I've had it put in joint names.' He gave a hollow laugh. 'Funnily enough, I was going to ask you to marry me tonight—if I thought you'd have me, after whatever was coming. I knew you were going to replay the last act, so to speak, but I never dreamt it could be this.' He smoothed the dress down over her hips, straightening it absently. 'I should have known the dream was too real. I've had it for seven years, since that birthday. It never changes. It also isn't a patch on the real thing.'

She stood on tiptoe and kissed him. 'I dream about you too, and I quite agree. Now, about going back to my place and——'

'No, Janna. Not until we're married.'

'Married!' she exclaimed. 'Finn, that'lll take ages!'

'No, it won't,' he said with a humourless chuckle. 'This must be the longest engagement on record, but I have no intention of letting it drag on any longer, now I know about it! You, young woman, are going to marry me just as soon as it can be arranged.'

'What about my father?' she asked.

Finn snorted. 'What about him? He's on my side—
he said weeks ago it was high time I made an honest
woman of you. I thought he was just joking. I don't
think you'll find he gives us any trouble at all!'

The little church was full to overflowing. Almost everyone on the peninsula was there, including Betty
Buchan, who was happy in her new home and much
less confused. She was sitting with Jessie McGregor,
and patting her eyes with a tissue.

'They make a fine couple, Jessie,' she said.

'Aye, they do.'

'Ye'll have those grandchildren now, ye ken.'

'Aye.'

'He's like your Dougal, Jessie. He would ha' been
proud of Finn.'

Jessie nodded. 'Aye, he would. He's his father's son,
right enough.'

'Mind,' Betty said in a stage whisper, 'it's a strange
thing to do, getting married in the middle of the
night. . .'

Christmas Journeys

4 new short romances all wrapped up in 1 sparkling volume.

Join four delightful couples as they journey home for the festive season—and discover the true meaning of Christmas...that love is the best gift of all!

A Man To Live For - Emma Richmond

Yule Tide - Catherine George

Mistletoe Kisses - Lynsey Stevens

Christmas Charade - Kay Gregory

Available: November 1995   **Price: £4.99**

MILLS & BOON

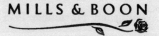

MILLS & BOON

CHRISTMAS CRACKERS

A cracker of a gift pack full of
Mills & Boon goodies. You'll find...

Passion—in *A Savage Betrayal* by Lynne Graham

A beautiful baby—in *A Baby for Christmas* by Anne McAllister

A Yuletide wedding—in *Yuletide Bride* by Mary Lyons

A Christmas reunion—in *Christmas Angel* by Shannon Waverly

Special Christmas price of 4 books
for £5.99 (usual price £7.96)

Published: November 1995

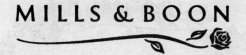

MILLS & BOON

LOVE CALL

The books for enjoyment this month are:

A FAMILIAR STRANGER	Caroline Anderson
ENCHANTING SURGEON	Marion Lennox
DOWNLAND CLINIC	Margaret O'Neill
A MATTER OF ETHICS	Patricia Robertson

Treats in store!

Watch next month for the following absorbing stories:

DR WENTWORTH'S BABIES	Frances Crowne
CRISIS IN CALLASAY	Drusilla Douglas
A PROMISE TO PROTECT	Abigail Gordon
A TEMPORARY LOVER	Carol Wood

Available from W.H. Smith, John Menzies, Forbuoys, Martins,
Tesco, Asda, Safeway and other paperback stockists.

Readers in South Africa - write to:
IBS, Private Bag X3010, Randburg 2125.

A years supply of Mills & Boon Romances — absolutely free!

Would you like to win a years supply of heartwarming and passionate romances? Well, you can and they're FREE! All you have to do is complete the wordsearch puzzle below and send it to us by 30th April 1996. The first 5 correct entries picked after that date will win a years supply of Mills & Boon Romance novels (six books every month — worth over £100). What could be easier?

STOCKHOLM	PARIS	HELSINKI	ANKARA
REYKJAVIK	LONDON	ROME	AMSTERDAM
COPENHAGEN	PRAGUE	VIENNA	OSLO
MADRID	ATHENS	LIMA	

N	O	L	S	O	P	A	R	I	S
E	Q	U	V	A	F	R	O	K	T
G	C	L	I	M	A	A	M	N	O
A	T	H	E	N	S	K	E	I	C
H	L	O	N	D	O	N	H	S	K
N	S	H	N	R	I	A	O	L	H
E	D	M	A	D	R	I	D	E	O
P	R	A	G	U	E	U	Y	H	L
O	A	M	S	T	E	R	D	A	M
C	R	E	Y	K	J	A	V	I	K

Please turn over for details on how to enter ➡

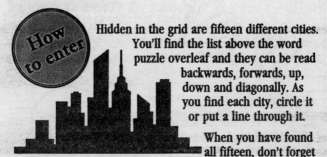

How to enter

Hidden in the grid are fifteen different cities. You'll find the list above the word puzzle overleaf and they can be read backwards, forwards, up, down and diagonally. As you find each city, circle it or put a line through it.

When you have found all fifteen, don't forget to fill in your name and address in the space provided below and pop this page in an envelope (you don't need a stamp) and post it today. Hurry – competition ends 30th April 1996.

Mills & Boon Capital Wordsearch
FREEPOST
Croydon
Surrey
CR9 3WZ

Are you a Reader Service Subscriber?   Yes ☐   No ☐

Ms/Mrs/Miss/Mr _____

Address _____

_____

_____ Postcode _____

One application per household.

COMP495
D

mps
MAILING
PREFERENCE
SERVICE